Christy's Love

Maud Johnson

SCHOLASTIC INC.
New York Toronto London Auckland Sydney Tokyo

ISBN 0-590-33096-9

Copyright © 1984 by Maud Johnson. All rights reserved. Published by Scholastic Inc.

12 11 10 9 8 7 6 5 4 3 2   4 5 6 7 8 9/8

Christy's Love

A Wildfire® Book

WILDFIRE® TITLES FROM SCHOLASTIC

O^{ne}

On Christmas morning I was watching for Mike, trying not to be obvious about it although I deliberately chose a chair near the window of the den, and as his car came up our hill I grabbed my coat and ran outside. The December cold was penetrating despite the sunshine, and a gusty wind blew my hair away from my face. In the distance the tops of the Blue Ridge Mountains were crusted with snow.

Mike circled the house and stopped his car in the backyard, just as I expected. I waited on the next-to-bottom step, smiling because the sight of him gave me a lovely feeling.

"Hi, there," he called and grinned, walking toward me. "Merry Christmas, Christy." In his left hand he had three packages wrapped in shiny red paper.

"Merry Christmas to you," I told him.

"You're very punctual. Last night you said you'd be here by eleven, and —" I consulted my watch, "it's exactly one minute until eleven." It wasn't important, just something to say while we smiled at each other.

Mike was taller than I, but when he stood on the ground and I remained on the step, our faces were level, his breath fanning my cheeks. He stared at my mouth and I knew he wanted to kiss me, and I wanted him to do it, but not there in the bright sunshine with both my parents in the den, which had a bay window facing the backyard. Mama and Dad didn't spy on me and they had to know Mike and I exchanged kisses, but I would have died of embarrassment if a boy — even Mike Maxwell — showed that much affection in front of my family.

Mike understood. His gaze moved from my lips to my eyes. "Know something, Christy?" he asked softly.

"What?"

"I'm very, very glad you're my girl. Here —" he extended the packages. "For you."

"Mine for you are in the house. Come on in." I turned and started up the steps. "Mike, didn't we decide to give each other only two gifts? You have three boxes."

"Good grief! I do, don't I?" He pretended to be astonished. "Maybe I can't count."

Both of us laughed. I wondered how anyone in the whole wide world could be as happy as I felt at that moment.

Mike poked his head in the den doorway to speak to Mama and Dad, admired our Christmas tree that he'd helped me trim two nights earlier, and smiled again as I took two gaily wrapped boxes for him from the hall closet. We went into the kitchen and stopped beside the table that was placed to have a wide view of the Blue Ridge through the bay window, only for once, neither of us paid attention to the mountains. Our kitchen had a Christmassy smell that morning with the turkey roasting in the oven and the candied yams giving off the scent of cinnamon and brown sugar. Two mincemeat pies Mama baked after breakfast were cooling on the counter.

Mike insisted that I open my gifts first. The big package was a photograph album for snapshots, something I'd said I wanted, and the second one held a white sweater.

"Mike, this sweater is gorgeous!" I exclaimed. "I never felt anything so soft. And it's the right size, too."

"I phoned your mother to find out the size," he grinned. "Open the last one, Christy."

I caught my breath as I took the lid off the third box and removed a slim gold bracelet. It was so beautiful I was speechless.

"Well, do you like it?" he asked.

"Like it? Oh, Mike —" I slipped the golden circle on my wrist and held my hand in the sun, seeing the bracelet sparkle. "I adore it."

"Do you 'adore' it enough to kiss me?"

His voice was light but his eyes were serious. I stood on tiptoes to put my arms around

3

him. The kiss was long and sweet.

"Open your packages, Mike," I said finally, breaking the embrace. "And if you like your gifts as much as I like mine, maybe you'll show your appreciation by returning that kiss."

He ripped the glittery paper. The larger box had a pair of dark brown leather gloves and a cashmere muffler in a rich blue-gray shade — the exact smoky color of his eyes and of the Blue Ridge Mountains on a clear day. He exclaimed over both, immediately placing the muffler around his neck and trying on the gloves.

"I didn't have to call your mother," I said. "Your hand is about the same size as my dad's, so I asked him what size he wore."

"They're great. Really great, Christy. But you acted sort of annoyed because I had three gifts for you, and you bought three for me. A scarf plus gloves adds up to two in my book even though they were in one box."

"Maybe I can't count, either," I came back and giggled. "Open the small package."

His other present was a silver key chain with his initials engraved on a flat silver disc about the size of a nickel. From the expression on his face I could tell he was pleased.

"This has real class," he said, turning the chain over in his hand. "I never owned anything with my monogram." Looking at me, he smiled tenderly. "Remember that kiss we talked about a moment ago?"

"Oh — that?" I shrugged as if it wasn't

4

important. He knew I was teasing. "I —"

Whatever I was about to say was never spoken because Mike's arms went around me and his mouth came down firmly on mine. I could feel his heart thumping against my chest, or maybe I heard my own heartbeats while we clung together.

The sound of laughter from the den brought us back to reality and to the fact that although we might be alone at the moment, we weren't completely by ourselves. My mother's footsteps indicated she was walking down the hall, humming "Deck the Halls with Boughs of Holly," and as Mike and I moved apart, it dawned on me she was letting us know she was headed for the kitchen.

"Mike, Christy tells me you're having a family gathering at your house today," she said as she opened the oven door to peek at the turkey.

"We sure are, Mrs. Jamison," he answered. "Neither of my brothers can come but Mom's sister and her husband and their twins from Richmond are here for the day, and Uncle Eb will eat dinner with us. I'd better get going, too. I had my orders that I'm to keep those ten-year-old twins occupied between noon and one o'clock so Mom can get the food on the table." He turned to me. "Christy, I'll see you this afternoon when the relatives leave. Okay?"

Murmuring, "Fine," I walked to the door with him. He gave my fingers a little squeeze and bounded to his car.

T*wo*

My father worked for a company that manufactured electric motors, and he was transferred so often that we had lived in several states by the time he was sent to Greenview, Virginia, a small town in sight of the Blue Ridge Mountains. Going to Greenview was a promotion for him since he would manage the company plant there, but we'd only been in New York State a year and I hadn't wanted to move again so quickly. Changing high schools in the middle of my junior year promised to be a nightmare, and I cringed at the prospect of once again trying to get settled in an unfamiliar house in an unfamiliar community. Making new friends, or trying to do it, can be a slow ordeal, and I'd braced myself for a lot of loneliness.

I did have lonely times at first, but eleven months after our arrival in Virginia, Greenview truly had become home, something I thought about on Christmas Day as I watched Mike drive down our hill. The majestic beauty of the mountains that rimmed the horizon on every side made me wonder how I'd ever considered flat land to be beautiful. I liked Greenview High and liked the other students — most of them — and best of all, Mike was now part of my life. If Dad hadn't been transferred to Virgina, I would never have known Mike Maxwell.

Our house was located two miles from town, a tall, skinny Victorian structure set in a grove of trees on top of a hill with a curved drive winding up from the highway. The two-story house was painted white with dark green trim, and it had nine bay windows that provided every room, even the kitchen, with a broad view of the Blue Ridge. "Crazy windows," Mike called the three-sided bays, but he liked them as much as I did.

The first time I saw Mike was the day after we reached Virginia when Mama and I went to the grocery store and then stopped to buy gasoline at the service station that was owned and operated by Eben Maxwell, Mike's uncle. Mike worked there after school, on Saturdays, and in the summer. We knew nothing about the Maxwells then, and the only reason my mother went to that particular place was that we needed gas and saw the service station sign.

A tall, lanky boy with brown hair and smoky blue-gray eyes cleaned the car windshield while the tank was filling. He looked to be about my age or slightly older, and on that frigid January afternoon he was bundled up in a heavy khaki jacket and a black knitted cap, his face ruddy from the cold.

Mama was behind the steering wheel and I sat on the front seat beside her. The boy started a conversation with me by saying he'd seen our New York license tags and wondered if we were tourists just passing through. When I explained about our moving, he asked if I would be going to Greenview High. I said yes.

"Then I'll see you at school." He smiled, his teeth very white. "I go there, too."

I was drawn to him instantly but was so shy around boys that I didn't tell him my name or find out his, and I hated myself for not being more outgoing. Thinking about it a few days later, though, I realized it probably wouldn't have mattered what I said that first afternoon because at school I learned he was Mike Maxwell, a popular guy and, like me, a junior. I also discovered he went steady with Jill Rogers, the most beautiful girl in high school. She had gold-flecked auburn hair and a gorgeous figure with curves in all the right places, and merely thinking about her made me feel drab. I kept my brown hair shiningly clean, but it didn't have the radiance hers had, and my figure was slim, almost boyish compared to hers.

Mike and I had a few classes together, and we spoke when we passed in the hall at school

8

— if he wasn't with Jill and so engrossed in whatever she was saying he couldn't notice anything or anybody else. During my first three months in Virginia I tried to content myself with secret daydreams about him, never daring to hope he would look at me twice except to say hello.

The miracle happened in April after he broke up with Jill. He began dating me.

We had a marvelous summer and when classes started in the fall, we were seniors and everyone knew I'd become "Mike's girl." We saw a lot of Betsy Collins and Gordon Sager who, like us, went steady, and Bud Warren, Mike's next-door neighbor. All of them were seniors and long-time friends of Mike's, accepting me quickly because I was Mike's girl. The loneliness I'd experienced when my family first moved south was long gone, and best of all, Mike, the boy I loved, also loved me.

It's odd how life can change so gradually you never realize what's happening until everything is different. During the summer and autumn Mike and I disagreed a few times, but never about important topics, just about silly matters, his liking a certain TV show I found dull or where we'd go for a picnic. We didn't have a real quarrel until two weeks before Christmas — maybe *quarrel* is the wrong word since we didn't scream at one another or make ugly cracks. I was so naive I didn't realize we would have been better off talking about the situation, but we didn't do that and what began as a small misunderstanding grew and grew until it was monstrous.

A big part of it was my fault, but Mike wasn't entirely blameless. I had a job for Saturdays and the Christmas holidays at Carlyle's Gift Shop, and although Mike was thrilled for me when I was hired, after a time he appeared bored if I mentioned my work. He seldom had much to say about what he did at the service station, but I suppose he hated my having any activity I liked that excluded him.

There was another angle he never pinpointed although I could sense it: He took a dim view of my working relationship with Lee Carlyle, the son of the gift-shop owner. Lee, a good-looking blond boy who went to a nearby community college, helped out in the shop, working mostly in the stockroom. I felt it was ridiculous for Mike to be jealous of Lee, and then all of a sudden I learned firsthand about jealousy when Mike gave Jill Rogers a ride home one December afternoon.

Mike always picked me up at six o'clock when the gift shop closed, and that day I reached his car to find Jill sitting beside him. She was in the middle of the front seat, her leg pressing against Mike's, and she and I spoke coolish greetings. Ignoring me, she didn't move an inch. I waited, standing in the street, expecting her to get out so I could get in and take my customary seat next to Mike or for him to say something like, "Scoot over, Jill," but nothing happened. She remained in the middle, inching even closer to him, if possible. I sat down, finally, and was against the door on the passenger side.

Maybe it was a little thing, but Jill knew I was dating Mike and *I* knew *she* would like to date him again and her actions made me angry. She was beautiful and sexy, traits I didn't feel I had, and I was terrified for fear that Mike's being with her for just that short a time might make him decide he preferred dating her to me. It wasn't that I didn't trust Mike, but Jill Rogers had the ability to attract boys merely by smiling at them, and she flirted outrageously with Mike on the way to her house that evening.

As soon as she was out of the car, Mike and I had words about it. He accused me of being overly possessive if I didn't want him to give a friend a ride, and both of us were livid as he drove up my hill. The second he stopped at my house, I flounced out of his car and he zoomed off in a huff.

I was too upset about all of it to eat any dinner or carry on a conversation with my parents that night, and for the first time in months Mike didn't phone or show up at my door. Hurt, fear, and anger were jumbled together inside me until I felt physically sick. I was positive he was with Jill — something that didn't happen, I learned later. The following evening when I still hadn't heard from him after a long, long night and day, I accepted a date with Lee Carlyle to go to a party.

The party was a disaster for me. Lee's friends were older, all of them in college, and my shyness returned when they teased me after discovering I wasn't out of high school. But the real reason I had such an unhappy time was because I wasn't with Mike. I realized it, and also realized that if Mike and I didn't make peace quickly, we might never do it.

I apologized first. The following day I went to Mike and said I was sorry. He apologized, too, the misery etched on his face matching mine and letting me know he'd been as distressed as I was. We went into each other's arms, sharing the sweetest kisses in the world, and everything was right once more. Both of us promised to talk out our troubles in the future — if we ever had troubles again.

If is a big word to have only two letters. Mike and I were close once more, together as often as possible. I couldn't imagine anything ever being as awful as the time we were not speaking.

I wonder what I'd have thought on Christmas morning if I had known about the future when I stood at our back door to watch Mike's car going down the hill, the sunlight glinting on my new bracelet. I would never have believed what was about to happen in less than a week.

Three

It was almost four o'clock when Mike returned to my house Christmas afternoon. He was wearing the muffler and gloves I'd given him, and he grinned in approval when he saw I had on the white sweater. Both of us had changed our good clothes for jeans, but the new bracelet hadn't been off my wrist.

"Did you survive those ten-year-old twins?" I asked him.

"I gave them the workout of their lives. Do you want to go outside for a little while, Christy? I need to walk off my dinner."

"So do I," I admitted. "I'm not accustomed to such a big meal in the middle of the day. Where do you want to walk?"

"Anywhere. We shouldn't go far because dark comes early this time of year. Wrap up well, Christy. It's awfully cold."

Our feet crunched on the hard-packed

brown stubble of grass as we crossed the yard. Mike was right about the temperature, and even though the wind had died, the air was much colder than it had been in the morning. The lower rim of the sun was behind the blue mountains, the western sky splashed with coral and gold, and the leafless trees surrounding the house were tall silhouettes.

The level area on top of our hill sloped down behind the house with a wide dirt path leading past the outcropping of rocks that formed a stone bench. The bench was where Mike and I sat so many warm evenings to kiss and talk and count the stars. Farther along, on the opposite side of the path, we came to the cleared place where Mama had her garden. Mike paused there, scanning the bleak rectangle of nothingness that had been lushly thick with vegetables and flowers the previous summer.

"Is your mother planning another garden this summer?" he asked.

"Is she ever! She can't wait to start digging." I laughed softly. "She commented the other day that the one good thing about January is receiving seed catalogs in the mail."

"She'd need a blow torch to make a dent in this ground now and it's going to be frozen a long time yet." Mike stubbed at the dirt with the heel of his boot. "Christy, do you remember that Saturday last April when I plowed the garden for her?"

His voice was unexpectedly low. I looked

up at him to find he was gazing at me, each of us misty-eyed with the same memories.

"I'll never forget that day," I whispered.

Before the April plowing episode I'd had one date with Mike — just one — and I was crushed as well as embarrassed that he made no effort to date me again. Apparently he and Jill were feuding when he asked me to go out that one Friday evening, and they made up quickly because the following Monday they were holding hands at school. Mike's and my relationship reverted to hellos and some casual conversations while we waited for classes to begin. It hurt, and I told myself to face the fact that I wasn't cute enough to attract a boy like Mike, something difficult to swallow when I cared so much for him.

Mike's Uncle Eb found a man to plow Mama's garden in April, but the man didn't come and Mr. Maxwell sent Mike to our house to do it. Mike arrived on a Saturday afternoon in the service station truck with a small tractor attached to a hitch on the rear bumper. Self-consciousness surged through me at the sight of him because I was unable to stop thinking about the humiliation of one date and no follow-up, and I almost died when my mother insisted on my carrying a Coke to the garden for him. She made me take one for myself, refusing to allow me to beg off, and I trudged across the yard, the two red and white Coke cans frosty to my fingers. I was afraid that Mike would think

I was running after him, or that he was in a hurry to finish so he could leave, or worse, that he'd simply ignore me.

It wasn't that way at all. He couldn't have been more friendly. We chatted and laughed, and I forgot to be shy or ill at ease. When he asked if I'd like to ride the tractor with him, I said yes, climbing on the bucket seat to sit between his legs with his arms on either side of me so I wouldn't fall, ignoring the dust swirling about us and the uncomfortable perch because I'd never had more fun. That night Mike made a definite break with Jill, and the next day he came to my house again. We'd dated ever since except for the time during the pre-Christmas quarrel.

Both of us relived the April episode on Christmas afternoon as we looked at what used to be the garden. I glanced at Mike again. A funny little half smile curved at his mouth.

"Seems impossible we've only been going together since April, doesn't it?" he murmured. "Just eight months. I feel as if I've loved you all my life, Christy."

"I know. . . . That's how it is with me, too."

I leaned against his shoulder, knowing he was going to kiss me, and he did. As the long embrace ended we giggled at the coldness of each other's lips.

My parents were invited to an informal buffet supper at the home of friends Christmas night, and they were ready to go when Mike and I reached the house.

"You two have roses in your cheeks and sparkles in your eyes from the cold," Mama announced as if we'd been kindergartners, looking from Mike to me.

If my eyes are sparkling it's because of Mike's kisses, I thought, not saying it aloud.

"Christy, Betsy Collins phoned and wants you to call her right away," my mother went on. "I sliced some turkey so you and Mike can make sandwiches whenever you're hungry, and there's a whole mincemeat pie left."

"Mrs. Jamison, I knew it was smart for me to walk off my dinner," Mike said and grinned. "Your cooking is the greatest." The way he spoke made my parents laugh. Mike had a tremendous appetite and never turned down food, always praising things Mama prepared. Yet he never gained weight. He was tall, six feet, two inches, and could have comfortably used several more pounds without being fat.

"One more thing," Mama added as Dad held her coat. "Don't forget that tomorrow is a school day."

"School on the twenty-sixth of December — ugh," Mike groaned.

That was my reaction, too. The Greenview High School furnace had broken early in the month, and our classes were dismissed for Christmas at that time since a completely new heating system had to be installed. But instead of giving students extra holidays, the school board ruled that the lost days would be made up by having us return the day after Christmas rather than on the second of January. In addition, we faced Saturday classes for four weeks.

I didn't dislike school and probably would have been ready to go back if I hadn't worked at the gift shop every day except Sundays right through Christmas Eve. I'd have loved a couple of days to do nothing but sleep, eat, and be with Mike. My mother knew Mike and I hadn't forgotten about the twenty-sixth. Reminding us was her way of telling him he couldn't stay late on a school night. She and Dad were strict about that.

We went into the den where our phone was located. Mike picked up a magazine while I dialed the Collins' number.

"Merry-End-of-Christmas and all that good stuff," Betsy said. "If you and Mike don't have big plans for tonight, Gordon and I thought we'd come over."

"Love to see you," I answered.

"Did you hear the news about school?"

"Have our classes tomorrow been postponed?"

Mike, sitting a few feet from me, jerked his eyes away from the magazine when he heard me ask that question.

"No such luck, but we do get New Year's Day as a holiday," she said. "It's to be announced officially tomorrow, but my dad heard it last night from Mr. Crenshaw who is on the school board. It seems the board is afraid a lot of students will cut classes New Year's Day if they partied on New Year's Eve even though they know they'll get F's for cutting during the makeup days."

"Won-der-ful." I stretched the word out.

"Gordon and I have decided to have a New Year's Eve party, and you and Mike are invited. My parents said we can have it here if everybody agrees not to stay too late."

"We accept and we'll leave on time. See you and Gordon later."

Mike listened eagerly as I repeated what Betsy had said, his eyes glistening when he heard about the holiday and the party. He didn't like great mobs of people, but he genuinely enjoyed being with friends.

Bud Warren came to my house Christmas night with Betsy and Gordon, explaining that he'd been killing time by walking around the block when they passed him.

"They told me where they were heading and asked if I wanted to tag along, so here I am," Bud said.

"The more the merrier," I came back and meant it.

"Was Santa good to you this year, Bud?" Mike inquired.

"You bet. Mom found a catalog for electronics and ordered a bunch of gadgets for me, so I have plenty to do figuring them out. Dad came through with cash. Very welcome." He patted the wallet in his hip pocket.

"Did your grandmother knit you another sweater?" Betsy asked and giggled.

Bud always had funny stories to tell about his grandmother who was in her eighties and lived in a condo in New Jersey, spending her days knitting and her nights playing bridge.

"Of course." Bud rolled his eyes. "One year the sweater she makes me is too small, so the next year she thinks big and knits big. You ought to see what she sent this time. It could hold Siamese twins."

Everyone laughed. Bud was a likable boy with a warm personality, which was fortunate as he was painfully homely with protruding ears and a head too small for his sturdy body. His thin, straw-colored hair grew in every direction no matter how hard he tried to train it, the pale hair an odd contrast to his dark, bushy eyebrows. Mike, Gordon, and some of the other guys tried to look out for him, and I'd often wondered if it was because of his appearance, although after I came to know him well, I seldom thought about his looks.

Bud dated a little but didn't go steady, and it was no secret that he'd always been wild about Jill Rogers. Mike thought Bud's feelings for Jill were genuine and also that it boosted Bud's ego to be with a girl as beautiful as she was. Jill used him, another trait of hers that I disliked, as she would break dates with Bud if someone she considered more interesting asked her to go out. Sometimes when she had no plans for a specific evening and didn't want to stay home alone, she'd call Bud, and he went running to her like an obedient puppy dog.

It must have been hard on Bud when Jill and Mike were going steady. I asked Mike about that once, hearing him say, "It bothered me, too. I wouldn't hurt Bud for anything." He'd looked so troubled that I changed the subject. He and Bud had been good friends all of their lives.

Occasionally Betsy and I discussed Jill if we were alone, my comments guarded since Jill was once Mike's girl. Betsy wasn't a gossip, and I knew what I said to her wouldn't be repeated. I suppose the fellows talked about Jill, too, but she was one topic seldom mentioned in a mixed crowd.

Christmas evening Dad had built a fire on the den hearth, and after Betsy, Gordon, and Bud arrived, Mike put a fresh log on. The five of us watched the bright flames shoot up, the wood crackling until the blaze settled into red embers. We didn't talk about serious matters at first, just made silly cracks back and forth until Gordon mentioned college. An instant silence engulfed us. All of us had sent in college applications for the fall and were waiting to hear if we'd been accepted. It probably would be spring before we received word, a long time to wait to know something that would influence the rest of our lives.

Mike and I had saved the mincemeat pie for later after we filled up on turkey sandwiches, and when I went into the kitchen to serve it, Betsy came with me. I cut the pie into five slices.

"I don't know what to do about inviting Jill to the party," Betsy commented in an undertone so she wouldn't be overheard. "Gordon thinks we should include her and I don't want to hurt her feelings by leaving her out, but if she shows up with Carl Browning or some other thug. . . ." She let the sentence hang, unfinished.

"Why don't you include her and tell her Bud will stop for her?" I suggested. "You'd make his day."

"You know how Jill is, Christy. You can never count on how she'll act. If she came with Bud, she'd look over the party crowd and decide to make a dive for the best-looking fellow there whether he already had a date or not."

"That would be Mike — and she'd have to fight me off."

"I think it would be Gordon," Betsy chimed in quickly. "I think he's as handsome as you think Mike is, and if Jill tried to take Gordon away from me, I'd claw her eyes out!" She gave a giggle. "You and I sound awfully vicious, don't we?"

"That we do. I'm not worried about Mike, though." Glancing at my wrist, I looked lovingly at the gold bracelet, a token of Mike's love for me. "You and I are lucky, Betsy. I used to envy Jill because she could always 'get' a boy by tossing that auburn mane of hers and giving him a big smile, but sometimes now I feel sorry for her. She can attract guys with no apparent effort, but she can't hold on to one for long after she starts dating him — except for Bud. Bud is like a puppet with Jill pulling the strings and —"

"Hey — you out there!" Mike's voice rang out from the den. "What gives? Are you eating up all the pie without giving us any?"

"Come and get it," I replied, carefully lifting the fifth slice of pie to a plate. Betsy, who had been at my house enough to know her way around the kitchen, counted out five forks and five paper napkins.

An hour later they left. They'd just started down our hill when my parents turned off the highway, the two automobiles stopping side by side briefly. Mike and I watched from one of the bay windows in the front of the house, seeing beams from the headlights splash through the darkness.

"That's my cue to get my jacket before your mother drops another hint about this being a school night," he said. "I'll kiss you good-night first. It's better without your folks in the house."

It was, I agreed, a smart idea.

Mike usually drove me home from school in the afternoons before he went to work at the service station, but Dad insisted on my going on the school bus in the mornings to make sure I was there on time. The bus stopped at the foot of our hill.

On the morning of the twenty-sixth of

December, Mike was waiting where I knew he would be as the yellow bus came to a halt in the parking lot. He leaned against a corner of the school building, his books and loose-leaf notebook cupped in his left hand resting on his hip bone, the collar of his jacket turned up around the back of his neck. He looked solemn until he spotted me, and then he smiled, his breath a tiny curl of white steam in the frigid temperature.

"Hi, there," he said as he'd done so many other mornings.

"Hi, yourself."

He and I weren't alone. Other buses were unloading, and students milled around us. Everybody seemed to be talking at once.

"Do you feel intelligent?" I asked. "If you don't, you'd better think about it because exams start three-and-a-half weeks from now. I checked the calendar before I left home. Isn't that a jolly prospect?"

"Jolly?" He lifted his eyebrows. "My word for it is *gross*. You sure know how to ruin a day, Christy. You keep coming up with those profound goodies and I'll take you out in the country and hide you under a toadstool."

I burst out laughing at his answer. The first bell sounded, and we turned to go inside. Mike reached for my hand, his fingers circling mine until we separated at the foot of the stairs since we were in different homerooms. He gave me a final smile when he started down the long corridor while I headed for the second floor.

F*our*

On New Year's Eve I didn't begin to feel concerned about Mike until quarter to nine. Unless he had a very good reason, he was usually on time and when he drove me home from school that afternoon he said, "See you at eight tonight for the party, Christy." Betsy had told us the party started at eight.

"I'll be ready," I answered Mike as he braked the car at my house. "I have a new dress."

"Sounds interesting. What color?"

"Wait and be surprised, Mike Maxwell! I'll give you a clue, though. It goes perfectly with a certain gold bracelet, but then, everything goes with that bracelet."

His mouth curved into a smile. "You like it, huh?"

"Almost as much as I like you, Mike."

The tenderness in his eyes said, "I love

25

you," as plainly as if he'd uttered the words. It took all my willpower to make myself get out of his car. I knew he had to leave, but I never wanted him to go.

"Tell your Uncle Eb Happy New Year for me," I added. "I'll be ready at eight."

I was ready at half-past seven and joined Mama and Dad in the den. The new dress was sheer white wool, simply made with long sleeves and a stand-up collar, the material so lovely it didn't require any trimming. My parents weren't going out and they sat in their favorite places, Mama on the sofa and Dad in the green-striped wing chair, his feet on the ottoman. They were watching television so I sat down beside my mother to watch with them until Mike arrived.

The TV program ended at eight and several commercials came on. Dad, who had finished reading the newspaper and tossed it aside, picked up one section again and folded the sheets to expose the crossword puzzle, taking a pencil from the drawer of the table by his chair.

"You and Mike be careful tonight," he said. "A lot of weirdo drivers will be on the road. They always come out of the woodwork on New Year's Eve."

I resisted the impulse to say we weren't children who had to be reminded and that Mike was a very good driver, which my father already knew. Besides, we wouldn't be "on the road," just in the car long enough to go into town to Betsy's.

"Mike is always careful," I answered.

I glanced impatiently at my watch at quarter past eight, and again at eight-thirty. "I'll bet Mike's uncle sent him out in the tow truck," I mumbled, remembering our first date when I despaired of his showing up, only to find he'd been delayed helping to get a wrecked automobile off the highway.

Neither of my parents said anything, and I tried to concentrate on TV, having a hard time doing it. Several minutes later I was so fidgety I couldn't sit still. I went to the front door, stepping out on the porch for a better view of the hill. It was seven minutes to nine.

A blast of icy air hit me. After a quick look, I came indoors. There was a steady flow of traffic on the highway below our house, but no one was slowing to turn into our drive.

By nine o'clock I couldn't stand it any longer. "I'm going to call Mike," I said and dialed the number at his house. The telephone rang and rang before I remembered that his parents were out of town.

"Mr. and Mrs. Maxwell are in Pennsylvania," I said to Mama and Dad. "Mike told me yesterday they'd gone to see his brother, Jack, and would be home tomorrow night. I forgot it until now."

Before I'd spoken the last word, I was dialing the Greenview Service Station. Nobody answered there, either.

Mike wouldn't deliberately stand me up. I knew that. Still, he should have contacted me if he was to be late . . . to be *that* late. . . . I was stiff with emotion, part of it fright that something was wrong, and part of it anger at his odd thoughtlessness, which wasn't like him.

"Christy, do you want me to drive you to Betsy's?" Dad asked in an overly casual way. "Mike can join you there."

"Bryan, that's a super idea!" Mama burst out. "I'll wait here to tell Mike where Christy is."

I shook my head. Going to the party without Mike was unthinkable. "Thanks, but I know he'll be along soon," I said.

My parents exchanged looks that indicated they were as troubled as I was. Mumbling something about putting on fresh lipstick, I ran into the downstairs bathroom to be by myself for a minute. The reflection in the bathroom mirror showed my mouth to be drawn, and my eyes were uncommonly large. At half-past seven when I had come downstairs in my new dress, excited about going to the party, I'd felt bubbly, even felt beautiful, and those sensations showed. But now, I was a bundle of tension and that showed, too.

Mama and Dad were talking in low tones when I returned to the den and they stopped instantly, which let me know they must have been discussing Mike and me. A strange little nagging feeling put a hollow ache in the bottom of my stomach, and a thought I'd tried to avoid surfaced in my mind. If Jill Rogers had called Mike . . . and he had stopped for her to let her ride with us. . . .

He wouldn't, I told myself firmly. I knew he wouldn't.

When our phone rang at five minutes past ten o'clock, I jumped up to answer. "Mike?" I gasped instead of saying hello or giving the person on the other end of the line a chance to speak.

"I'd like to talk to Bryan Jamison," a man said. The voice was vaguely familiar although I couldn't place it. The man sounded hoarse as if he had a sore throat.

I extended the phone to Dad who said, "Jamison here," into the mouthpiece. Mama flicked the TV off so there was silence in the den while the unseen man apparently was speaking. Finally my father said, "How badly hurt?"

I heard rough breathing and realized the rasping sound came from me. My lungs were about to explode.

"Where did it happen?" Dad asked, and there was another endless silence while the man on the line spoke. "Yes, I'm sure she'll want to come. We'll be there shortly," he finished and put the phone back in its cradle.

His face was paler than my white dress as he looked at me. "That was Eben Maxwell," he said in a tightly controlled voice. "Mike has been in an accident, Christy, and he's hurt. He's in the hospital."

Mama reached out to put her arm around my shoulders. I hadn't realized I was trembling.

"Hurt much?" I managed. I couldn't take

29

it in. I had been afraid of an accident without really believing it would happen.

"Badly hurt," Dad replied. "He hasn't regained consciousness and Eben thought you might want to be there in case he does."

"In case he does?" The terrifying question burned my tongue. "Do you mean *he might not?*"

"I don't mean that at all, Christy. It was a bad choice of words on my part, so let's not borrow trouble. What Eben meant was that Mike hasn't regained consciousness yet. If you want to go to the hospital now, get your coat. Your mother and I will go with you."

I was too numb to think clearly. Mama took my coat from the hall closet, and she held my arm as we left the house. We were halfway to the car when we heard the phone ring.

"I'd better answer it," Dad said and ran back to unlock the door.

He was visible through the den window as he picked up the phone and held it to his ear. My mother and I stood where we were in the cold darkness.

"That was Betsy Collins," he explained, quickly rejoining us. "She wanted to know why you and Mike hadn't come to the party, Christy. I told her about Mike's accident and also told her not to let any of the party crowd go to the hospital tonight. Remind me to phone her as soon as we know a little more. I promised her one of us would get in touch with her by midnight."

As a rule, if I was in the car with both my

parents, they sat in front and I was on the backseat, but that night Mama stayed close to me and sat in the back, too. I was glad she did. None of us talked. I don't suppose it was more than a ten- or twelve-minute drive, but it seemed much longer.

The Greenview Hospital was a four-story building made of yellow brick with an ell at the rear that housed doctors' offices. That late, with visiting hours long over, the public parking lot was deserted. I was surprised when my father passed the area until I realized where he was heading. He stopped near a white neon sign that said "Emergency Entrance," and we walked through double doors made of plate glass into a small lobby.

A man in a long white coat was seated behind a waist-high counter that separated the emergency lobby from what appeared to be an office. He asked if he could help us.

"Eben Maxwell contacted us about his nephew, Mike Maxwell, who is a patient," Dad said.

"Mr. Maxwell is in the waiting room. First door on your right." The man pointed in that direction, and I started with my parents on either side of me.

Mike's uncle, a lanky man with curly gray hair and Mike's blue eyes, was the only person in the waiting room, and his face showed his concern. I'd often thought Mike seemed closer to his Uncle Eb than he was to his mother and father.

"How is Mike?" Mama asked at once.

"The doctors are with him now," Mr. Maxwell answered. "They haven't given me a full report, but Mike had a bad lick on the head and apparently there are some internal injuries. His left shoulder is broken. The other car rammed his on the driver's side, and Mike's left arm and shoulder must have caught the blow."

I opened my lips and closed them again, unable to speak.

"Have you seen him?" Mama went on. That was what I'd have asked if I'd been able to phrase the question.

"No. The ambulance brought him here before I was notified, and by the time I received the message and reached the hospital, he was in one of the treatment rooms. He still is, and —" Mr. Maxwell hushed as three people came into the waiting room and took seats in the far corner. They paid no attention to us.

"John Nichols is the doctor on duty in the emergency section tonight," Mike's uncle continued, "and I think he's the best in town, so Mike is in good hands. I've been trying to reach Ada and Tom — my brother and sister-in-law, Mike's parents — but haven't had any luck so far. They're in Pennsylvania with Jack, and I've called Jack's apartment several times without getting an answer."

We sat down, Mr. Maxwell on the straight chair where he'd been sitting when we came in. Dad pulled a similar chair forward, while Mama and I took seats on a brown plastic couch with chrome arm rests. It was a rectangular room with white walls and limp tan curtains hanging at the window, the furnishings practical rather than pretty. A fern in a green ceramic pot occupied half a table, and some dilapidated magazines were stacked on the other half. A large framed photograph of the Blue Ridge Mountains hung on the wall opposite me. I stared at it just as I'd taken in the furniture, as though that might stop me from thinking of Mike.

The sound of an ambulance siren outside made all of us glance toward the lobby, which was visible through the open door of the waiting room. The screeching noise stopped, and several men came down the hall with a patient on a stretcher. The man in the white coat who'd met us in the lobby was with them.

"Another wreck, probably," Dad muttered. "Eben, do you know how Mike's accident happened?"

"Pete Powers was the state trooper who investigated, and he told me a little." Mr. Maxwell was as distraught as I felt. "Pete knows Mike and recognized him while he was lying in the wreckage before the rescue squad reached him, and Pete was the one who got in touch with me because he knew Mike works for me. Pete said there were several eye-witnesses and all of them gave the same report, that Mike had the right of way. He was just outside the city limits when it happened, on Church Street extension. There's a traffic light at Church and Hathaway, and Mike had the green and was into the intersection when this car came at him at right angles from Hathaway without slowing down. The other driver went through the red light, and Pete said he must have been doing at least seventy from the tire skid marks. He was drunk, so loaded he couldn't even give his name, and he wasn't hurt a bit. The front end of his car hit the side of Mike's, mashed in the door on the driver's side, and just sliced into Mike."

"What time was this?" Mama asked.

"About quarter to eight tonight." Mr. Maxwell reached into his coat pocket, taking out Mike's wallet and wristwatch. "The nurse gave me these." His voice broke. "The watch stopped at fourteen minutes to eight so that must be the time of the impact. I suppose Mike was on his way to get you, Christy. He told me this afternoon you two were going to a party."

The sight of Mike's belongings, the watch crystal shattered, did something to me. I began to cry.

I couldn't help it. Until that moment, I had been dry-eyed, too shocked to break down; but all of a sudden seeing that watch when Mike wasn't wearing it made something snap inside me. I pushed my head against Mama, sobs rocking my body. I wasn't screaming or making wild sounds, just weeping quietly with my face pressed into my mother's arm.

She held me, one of her hands sliding up and down my back. "Shhhh, Christy," she begged. "Please don't cry. Please. When you see Mike you don't want your eyes to be red and puffy, do you? It will upset him to find tear marks on your face."

I knew she was right and made a real effort to get myself together. She handed me some tissues from her coat pocket and asked Dad to see if he could find a cold cloth. Mike's uncle, commenting that he wanted to try the Pennsylvania number again, went to the pay phone beside the door.

Dad returned with several wet paper towels and I held them to my eyes. *I won't cry — I won't cry — I won't cry,* I told myself, hoping I could make the promise stick. Mr. Maxwell took his chair once more and said he'd had no luck with the phone call but would try once more after a while.

We didn't talk. Other people came and went, some of them as quiet as we were and others loud, their emotions raw. Apparently it was a busy time in the emergency department because I noticed nurses and doctors hurrying in the hall.

Shortly before midnight the man in the long white coat who had met us when we arrived came into the waiting room and for the first time I saw he wore a name tag pin that read: David R. Webster. He reminded me a little of Lee Carlyle, about the same age, twenty-one or twenty-two, and he had Lee's fair coloring.

He addressed Mr. Maxwell, but he was speaking to my family, also. "Dr. Nichols sent you a message," he said. "Your nephew's internal bleeding has been stopped and an orthopedic surgeon is examining his shoulder."

"Is Mike conscious, Dr. Webster?" Mr. Maxwell asked.

"No, he isn't. Dr. Nichols said to tell you it will be at least another hour before he can give you a firsthand report. Incidentally, I'm not a doctor." He smiled after the last sentence and disappeared into the hall.

Dad asked if I'd like to phone Betsy, and I shook my head. "You do it," I told him. "I can't talk to anyone right now, but tell her I'll be in touch with her tomorrow."

"You folks don't have to wait here at the hospital," Mr. Maxwell said. "I plan to stay, but you probably want to go home and —"

"I don't want to leave without seeing Mike!" I interrupted him, prepared to sit in that waiting room for days if necessary.

Some of my numbness was wearing off and I tried to be realistic. Besides, thinking about the future was less painful than dwelling on the present. If Mike had as many injuries as we were being led to believe, he might miss a lot of school and would need to study hard in order to graduate with our class in June. I'd help him with lessons as soon as he was able to study, I decided. I could get his assignments from his teachers and read the textbooks to him. If one of his arms had to be broken, I was thankful it was his left since he was right-handed — I remembered how well I'd managed with my left arm in a cast and a sling after it was broken in August. Yet, I couldn't have managed so well alone. My parents were wonderful, and so was Mike.

A new couple came into the hospital waiting room, the woman crying quietly as I'd done earlier. Her husband talked to her as he guided her to a seat. I shifted my position on the uncomfortable plastic couch, not wanting to stare at them.

"Eben, do you know the man who hit Mike?" Dad asked.

"Pete Powers gave me his name, but I've never heard of him. He lives on the other side of the county seat. A man in his fifties, Pete said, and that's old enough for him to have had more sense than to drink and drive. Well," Mr. Maxwell's mouth twisted, "he's going to wake up tomorrow with more trouble than a hangover when he finds himself in jail and tries to raise bond money and hears the charges against him."

But that won't help Mike, I thought. It wouldn't spare Mike any pain.

We were silent again. Time inched by. One o'clock in the morning on New Year's Day, one-fifteen. . . . At twenty-five minutes to two a nurse came to the waiting room door and said Dr. Nichols would see us in an office across the hall.

Mike's uncle made the introductions. Dad had met Dr. Nichols previously, but Mama and I hadn't — although I was familiar with his name since his son, Ralph, was in several of my classes. Dr. Nichols was a stocky man with a crisp black moustache and he was still wearing his loose green operating-room clothes, a white surgical mask dangling on his chest with the mask strings tied at the back of his neck.

"Mike's condition is critical," he said without wasting time on pleasantries. "He has a concussion and hasn't regained consciousness, although at the moment we're more concerned about the internal problems. There has been a lot of internal bleeding and I think it's under control, but if it starts again we'll have to go in to stop it, and we don't want to put him through surgery right now if that can be avoided. His left shoulder and arm are broken and they're packed in ice at the present to reduce swelling. There's a deep laceration on the left side of his face from his eyebrow down his cheek, but luckily, his eye wasn't touched. That laceration required stitches and in the future may require some plastic surgery to hide the scar, but that's not important at the moment. Getting him stabilized is. He's on oxygen, and we have a respirator standing by if he needs it."

The doctor paused and waited. Nobody spoke.

"What about Mike's parents?" he asked.

Mr. Maxwell explained why they weren't at the hospital. "I expect it will be some time tomorrow afternoon at the earliest before they reach Greenview. The Jamisons —" he looked at us, "are very good friends of Mike's. Especially Christy. I guess if Mike is allowed to see anyone, he'll want to see her."

"He'll be transferred to Intensive Care on the fourth floor in a very few minutes. You people can have a quick look at him now if you want," Dr. Nichols replied. "He's not conscious, so there won't be any communication with him, but you can speak to him if you want. Sometimes a supposedly unconscious person will recognize a voice or subconsciously take in a remark made in his presence, so don't say anything you wouldn't want him to hear if he were alert. Don't go in there and say, 'Doesn't he look awful?' or, 'Is he dead?' or that sort of thing. Above all, don't cry or moan. If you did and he was aware of it, even though he couldn't acknowledge what was happening, it would upset him and he has enough problems without any extras."

Maybe Dr. Nichols suspected that I'd cried in the waiting room. I didn't know if my eyes were still red or not, but I made up my mind to show no emotion around Mike except love and tenderness.

We made a procession along the corridor, Dr. Nichols and Mr. Maxwell in front, then Mama and me, with Dad at the rear. Dr. Nichols led us through a door marked "No Admittance — Employees Only," and into a white-tiled room where a nurse was standing beside a bed. I caught my breath. The figure on the bed was Mike, although I might not have recognized him if I hadn't known he would be there.

He lay very still, more like a gray plaster mannequin than a human being. A white gauze bandage covered part of his forehead and his left cheek. Below the bandage, a scabby scrape that was painted with some kind of medicine made his left jaw an orange-red while the rest of his skin, instead of being its normal ruddy tan, was completely without color. His left arm was wrapped in what appeared to be bulky layers of opaque plastic. The ice pack, I decided.

There were tubes everywhere, the oxygen tube clamped under his nose, another tube down his throat, one coming from under the sheet draining into a plastic bottle taped to the side of the bed. His right hand was strapped to a board about eight inches long with needles going into his arm so blood and clear liquid could drip into his veins from two bottles suspended on poles attached to the top of the bed.

I wanted to reach my hand out and touch him, and there was no place to touch. But I had to let him know I was with him. I had to.

Taking a step forward, I said, "Mike, it's Christy. You're going to be fine. Just fine." My voice was amazingly steady, considering the way my heart pounded, but I was quivering inside. Tears stung my eyes and I blinked them away. I had no intention of breaking down again unless I was somewhere other than the hospital.

The man named David Webster came into the room. Dr. Nichols said something to the nurse, and she and Mr. Webster began to wheel Mike's bed toward the elevator.

Mike, I thought desperately, *Mike, I love you.*

"I have a boy Mike's age and I can imagine what you people feel." The doctor's voice was soft.

"That's Ralph, isn't it?" I asked him. "I know Ralph at school and so does Mike."

"I hope there will be a better report in the morning," Dr. Nichols said. "Only family members are permitted to visit a patient in Intensive Care under most circumstances, but I'll leave an order that you, Christy, can see Mike if you're with his parents or with Eben — and if his parents don't object. You'll be allowed five minutes at noon and another five minutes at seven in the evening. Once he's out of Intensive Care and in a room, the visiting rules are more lenient."

"Dr. Nichols, does Mike hurt?" I seemed to be speaking from miles away. "What I mean is, when he wakes up, will he be in a lot of pain?"

"We have medications to keep him from suffering."

"He'll be all right, won't he?" I held my breath after asking.

"We'll do everything we can, Christy."

F*ive*

A sleety rain was falling New Year's morning when I went downstairs. Dad and Mama had finished eating but were still at the breakfast table in the kitchen and, like me, they had on robes. The first day of the year was a holiday for my father.

"Christy, I was hoping you'd sleep at least another hour since you were up so late last night," Mama said. The kitchen clock showed sixteen minutes to nine.

I murmured something about getting enough rest, which wasn't entirely the truth. It had been after two when Dad, Mama, and I left the hospital and I was so tired my body throbbed. But once we were at home, I was wakeful a long time, too keyed up to doze off. Every little noise made me twitch. Wind rattled the tree branches, and our house always groaned and creaked in the night if there was much difference in the indoor and outside temperatures.

After lying in bed for an eternity, I got up without turning on a light, wrapped a blanket around myself, and sat on the window seat. No stars showed and the sky was too black for me to make out the mountains. An occasional automobile came down the highway, its headlights disappearing around the bend in the road.

I wanted to stop thinking about Mike but couldn't, seeing him in my mind, remembering the pitiful way he looked on the hospital bed with all those tubes. I wanted to help him get well, wanted it desperately, and maybe it was selfish, but I needed him to comfort me. There was security for me in his arms. I wanted him to pull me close so I could nestle against him. I wanted to kiss him and have him kiss me.

Returning to bed after a while, I silently repeated poems I'd had to memorize in school until I became drowsy, although it was a strange, restless sleep filled with unsettling dreams. I woke up often and went back to sleep to dream again, until at last I opened my eyes to find muted daylight in the room. My watch had stopped because I had forgotten to wind it the night before, but I knew my parents were up as the scent of bacon and coffee came from the kitchen.

"What would you like for breakfast, Christy?" Mama asked.

"Nothing. I'm not hungry."

Her question sent a surge of anger over me. Didn't she know I had a lump in my throat the size of a walnut? How could she think of food when Mike was in the hospital?

Those unspoken thoughts might have made me smile if I hadn't felt so troubled about Mike. My mother always seemed to believe any problem could be solved with food or a cup of hot tea or a cold washcloth on the forehead.

She set a plate with a strip of bacon and a warm roll in front of me. "You need to eat," she said quietly. "You can't help Mike if you make yourself sick from worry and lack of nourishment." While she was speaking, she removed a carton of orange juice from the refrigerator and filled a glass for me.

"Is it too early to call the hospital?" I asked.

"Eben phoned here about thirty minutes ago to say he'd just spoken to one of the nurses in the Intensive Care section," Dad replied. "Mike's condition is unchanged."

"Then he isn't conscious?" I had the juice in my hand and set it on the table, not sure I could swallow.

"Apparently not or Eben would have mentioned it." Dad reached for the coffeepot and refilled his cup. "Eben was able to contact Mike's parents. Or rather, he spoke to Jack."

"When?"

"Not long after we left the hospital. It seems they had been out to celebrate the new year with some of Jack's friends, had come in, and were in bed by the time the call went through. Eben and Jack agreed it would be smart to let Mr. and Mrs. Maxwell have a few hours' sleep before starting to Virginia. Jack said he'd come with them and do the driving, then take a bus or plane back to Pennsylvania. That sounds like a good idea because the Maxwell family doesn't need another accident, and they might have had one rushing home if they'd left in the middle of last night with no rest."

"Mike's uncle is going to the hospital at noon today, isn't he?" I asked. *Please, please,* I begged silently. If he didn't go during the short visiting time, I wouldn't be allowed to see Mike since I wasn't a member of the family.

"Yes," Dad nodded. "Eben said he'd meet you on the fourth floor of the hospital a few minutes before twelve."

I tasted the juice, the cold liquid seeping down my throat, and because Mama was watching me without appearing to do it, I tried the bacon. It was crisp, just the way I liked it, and the roll was still warm. I had a taste and discovered I could chew as well as swallow. My mother, I decided, must be correct. Food, even a tiny bit of food, helped.

The hospital had a waiting room on the fourth floor, and I recognized some of the people who were downstairs the previous night. They apparently had friends or relatives in Intensive Care, too, and I hoped I didn't look as forlorn as most of them did.

Mike's uncle was there when my parents and I arrived. On any other day I'd have reminded my family that I had a driver's license and could get myself into town, but Dad and Mama seemed to take for granted that they'd come with me and, secretly, I was glad. If seeing Mike was especially upsetting, it might be difficult for me to concentrate on driving home alone.

At noon a nurse came into the waiting room and announced, "You may go in now, ladies and gentlemen. Please remember, just five minutes."

Mr. Maxwell stood up, but Mama and Dad didn't move. "All of you come on. You can be family today," Mike's uncle said to my parents. "And Christy, let's drop the 'Mr. Maxwell.' You can say Eben or call me Uncle Eb the way Mike does."

"All right, Uncle Eb." I could have told him I already called him that in my mind.

Intensive Care was a long room divided into cubicles with the beds placed at right angles against the walls. In the center, there was a series of tables for charts and equipment. Mike was just as he appeared at two o'clock in the morning when we saw him last, his skin still ashy, the tubes in place, his eyes closed. Nobody spoke at first, but I couldn't be silent. I had to let Mike know we were there even if he was unconscious. Maybe, as Dr. Nichols said, he would hear my voice and recognize it.

"Mike, it's Christy." I pronounced each word distinctly in case he was struggling to listen. "Your Uncle Eb and my parents are here, and I'm here, too. All of us are sorry you're hurt, but you're going to be all right. Just do everything the doctors and nurses tell you so you can be up and about soon."

I sucked my breath in, wanting to say more and unable to think of an appropriate remark except that I loved him, which was too personal to utter in front of my parents and Uncle Eb. "It's ugly outside," I added. "We have rain and sleet, and it's awfully cold. You chose the right day to be in bed."

I moved back, wishing he would flutter his eyelids or wiggle a finger, do anything to let me know he had heard. He didn't move. We stood beside him another minute and were about to go when Uncle Eb stepped closer to the bed.

"You hang in there, boy." His voice was gruff, his emotion showing. "A lot of folks are pulling for you, Mike. A whole lot."

Dr. Nichols was walking down the hall as we went toward the elevator. This time he had on a business suit instead of the green cotton shirt and trousers, and a stethoscope protruded from the side pocket of his coat.

"Have you seen Mike?" the doctor asked.

"Yes, we just left Intensive Care," Uncle Eb replied. "I couldn't detect any change."

"The internal bleeding hasn't resumed and that's a plus. Are his parents coming home today?"

Uncle Eb said yes. I decided the doctor's observation about the internal bleeding meant Mike was better and that made me feel better, too.

We had soup for lunch, made from the last of the Christmas turkey, and I discovered I actually was hungry. Mama beamed when I asked for a second helping.

Homework assignments for the following day had to be done in the afternoon, but before studying I phoned Betsy. Rather than using the den phone since Mama and Dad were there watching a football game on television, I went upstairs to use the extension in my parents' bedroom where I'd have more privacy.

It took a lot of effort for me not to think about how Mike and I would have spent the holiday if he hadn't been in the hospital. He probably would have eaten lunch at my house and maybe dinner. For a while he'd have watched football games with my father, the two of them speculating on why a quarterback called a particular play or how a tackle missed executing a block. I liked sports but wasn't as football-crazy as Mike although I watched the games whenever he did.

Betsy had a million questions. I answered as fully as I could, not leaving out any details about Mike's condition or the accident, my voice breaking from time to time. I was determined not to cry — and I didn't. Discussing all of it proved to be a strange sort of therapy for me as if talking lifted some of the misery.

"Oh, no!" she gasped when I described the way Mike looked. "Oh, Christy . . . how awful."

"Heaven knows how long it will be before he can go to school."

"Forget school. His getting well is more important."

"I know that. I was thinking about the fact that he might not be able to take his exams in two weeks. Betsy, I miss him so much I don't believe I can endure it."

"You'll have to be strong, Christy. Gee, who am I to be dishing out that kind of advice? I'd set a world's record for weepiness if Gordon had been hurt that badly."

I needed to change the subject and talk about other things. "How was your party?" I asked.

"Great at the beginning, but after you and Mike didn't show up, I figured there had to be trouble, that something was very wrong. When I called your house and Mr. Jamison told me about the wreck and said you and your mother were waiting for him to take you to the hospital — Christy, I nearly flipped. I told Gordon and he thought we should let the crowd at the party know, so he stood on a chair and whistled to get everyone's attention. You could have heard a pin drop after he explained what happened. The news really killed the fun because Mike is everybody's friend. People stayed on at my house until one o'clock, but it wasn't the same."

"You and Gordon should have another party as soon as Mike is on his feet. We'll come to that one."

"Will do. It's a promise. Tell Mike he's already invited, and let me know as soon as he can have visitors."

I assured her I would and we were ready to ring off when she thought of something else. "Hold on a sec, Christy." She gave a small giggle. "Jill was at the party, and you'll never guess the name of her date."

"Bud?"

"Try again."

"My brain isn't functioning enough for me to make any educated guesses today. Don't keep me in suspense."

"Vince Halloran."

Taking a huge breath, I was as surprised as Betsy thought I'd be. Jill had gone steady with Vince before she was Mike's girl, but Vince, who was supposed to have graduated the previous June, dropped out of high school in his senior year. He was failing and knew he wouldn't get a diploma, so he left Greenview before my family moved to Virginia, going to Ohio where his married sister lived.

I had met Vince when he returned to town to visit his mother, and Mike became furious back then because Vince asked me for a date I didn't accept. Vince was so handsome everyone thought he should be in the movies, and he and Jill were quite a pair together, both of them gorgeous. Vince Halloran might be handsome, but he wasn't as sweet or smart or likable as Mike in my opinion, and it had been ages since I'd thought of him except to assume he was still working in an appliance factory in Ohio.

"Is Vince back in Greenview for keeps?" I asked Betsy.

"No, he was just here over New Year's and he's probably left town by now. He told Gordon he had to be at work at seven tomorrow morning. You could have knocked me over with a feather when Jill showed up with him."

"Betsy, did it make Bud sick to find Jill with Vince?"

"At first, I thought it did. Bud had an odd expression on his face after he saw them arrive together, but he latched on to Kim Clark and sure didn't act as if he was grief-stricken over Jill."

"Kim Clark?" I couldn't believe it. Kim was a quietly pretty girl, nice, but Bud seemed to prefer vivacious people. I had a couple of classes with Kim but didn't know her well.

"When I invited Kim, she said she didn't have a date," Betsy went on. "I told her to invite a guy or get a ride with one of the couples, and she came with Nancy Holcombe and Freddie Stokes. Nancy is her cousin. But I'm positive Bud drove her home. He was by himself when he came, and every time I turned around, he was talking to Kim and both of them were smiling. She looked darling in a new blue dress and —"

Betsy stopped abruptly. I could hear her speaking to somebody in the room with her.

"Are you still there, Christy?" she came back on the line. "I have to go. My mother wants to use the phone. 'Bye for now."

Bud and Kim. I thought about that combination as I crossed the hall to my room and sat down at my desk to study. Kim was very shy, something I could understand as I'd been like that around boys until Mike became part of my life, and maybe dating Bud would do something wonderful for her. I hoped it would. As for Bud, if he became interested in a girl, really interested, he might get Jill out of his system once and for all.

Betsy's remark that Kim looked darling in a new dress rang in my ears. I wondered if I would ever be able to wear my new white dress again without reliving the horror of the night of Mike's accident.

When Dad, Mama, and I reached the hospital a little before seven that evening, Mr. and Mrs. Maxwell were in the waiting room with Uncle Eb and a tall fellow who had to be Mike's brother, Jack.

I knew Jack was sixteen years older than Mike, and Mike had told me once he almost felt as if he'd been an only child since both his brothers were grown and had left home before he was in grade school. His other brother, Louis, two years older than Jack, was a career Marine stationed on the West Coast. Jack looked enough like Mike to give me a start. He was Mike's height with the same lean build, and although his face was square and Mike's was more triangular, their coloring and features were similar. So were their blue-gray eyes.

I knew Mike's parents, but not nearly as well as I knew Uncle Eb, since we bought gas from Uncle Eb's service station and saw him often. Mike's father was a salesman for a farm equipment firm, and Mrs. Maxwell was secretary to a judge at the county courthouse located about twenty miles from Greenview. She was such a small woman I marveled that she could be the mother of three six-footers.

I had wondered many times if Mr. and Mrs. Maxwell were aware of the depth of Mike's and my relationship and that we genuinely cared for each other. But if they knew, they hadn't given any indication to me. Mike had eaten countless meals at our house, and months earlier it had surprised me that his mother had never asked me to join them, until I came to understand that they weren't a close family, not in the way my parents and I were close. Home to the Maxwells was chiefly a place to eat hurriedly, to sleep and change clothes, not a spot to relax and enjoy one another. Mike said they seldom sat down at the table together unless one of his brothers was visiting, or at a time like Christmas when relatives had been invited.

When the nurse came to the waiting room and announced that we could go into Intensive Care, Dad and Mama remained in their seats. Mr. and Mrs. Maxwell, Jack, Uncle Eb, and I trooped in. Mike's face looked just the same although his left arm and shoulder now were in a bulky plaster cast, and the tube had been removed from his mouth. The other tubes remained.

Mrs. Maxwell made a strangled sound when she saw him. I could imagine how shocked she must have felt since she hadn't been there the previous night. We stood around the bed, all of us staring at the still figure as if he were a marble statue.

"Christy," Mrs. Maxwell turned to me, "Eb tells me you've been talking to Mike in the hope that he might hear. What do you say to him?"

"Just — just that he isn't alone. That he's going to be all right. I don't know if he hears it or not."

She went to Mike and touched his right cheek with her fingers. "Dad and I came in from Pennsylvania a little while ago, Mike," she began. "We—" Her face crumpled and she pressed both hands to her mouth, turning toward her husband.

Jack completed the sentence for her, moving to the bed and saying something about the bad weather and heavy traffic. A nurse came to the cubicle and told us it was time to go.

Mr. and Mrs. Maxwell and Uncle Eb went

into the waiting room to speak to my parents once more. Jack and I waited in the corridor.

"I'm glad to meet you in person, Christy," Jack said, his grin so much like Mike's that my heart lurched. "Last summer when Mike went with me to Atlanta and we stopped at some of the Carolina beaches on our way back to Virginia, you were his main topic of conversation. We saw plenty of cute girls on the beach, but he didn't give them a second glance. That was when I figured you had to be special."

Blood rushed to my forehead at the compliment. "My parents and I were in Indiana visiting relatives while you and Mike made that trip," I murmured.

"He told me where you were. You'd written down your Indiana address for him, but he left it in his jeans and the washing machine took care of that piece of paper. Mike was really teed off at not being able to write or phone you."

I smiled at the memory, thinking how angry I had been at not hearing from him, and how lovely his kisses were after I came home and learned what happened.

"How long will you be in Greenview?" I asked Jack.

"Originally I planned to go tomorrow, but after seeing Mike and how badly he's hurt, I'm going to stay at least another forty-eight hours. Uncle Eb told me the injuries are major, but I wasn't quite prepared for this."

"Nobody was." My voice wavered.

"Mike's tough, Christy. He'll make it." Jack drew a deep breath. "I hope this emergency will be over in a hurry."

The word *emergency* made me shudder and an instant tightness in my throat left my mouth as dry as sandpaper. I couldn't have spoken at that moment if he'd asked me a direct question, but luckily, it wasn't necessary as the others joined us.

Mike's mother had herself under rigid control despite appearing pale, and I noticed that her husband kept a firm grip on her elbow. Uncle Eb patted me on the shoulder and when I looked up at him, he attempted to smile, not succeeding very well. I didn't succeed very well, either.

As we walked across the parking lot to our car, the cold air burned my lungs. The freezing rain had stopped, leaving a glaze everywhere, and icicles hung from the corners of the hospital building. Dad drove home cautiously, avoiding slick spots on the road, all of us silent.

"I don't plan to go to school tomorrow," I said as soon as we were in the house. "It's more important for me to go to the hospital to see Mike and —"

"Christy, that's out of the question!" my father barked.

"It certainly is," Mama echoed.

"But —"

She wouldn't let me finish. "Christy, Mike

will be in the hospital a long while, and you can't stay away from classes until he's well, especially with exams so near."

"But even if he's not conscious yet, five minutes with him is so short!" Panic made my voice thin. "If I don't see him at noon, I won't have a chance to be with him until tomorrow night at seven! Please! I'll keep up with my schoolwork! I promise I will!"

My parents exchanged their special glances, a private way they had of communicating without words. I'd wished many times I could read their minds when they addressed one another like that.

"What class do you have just before noon?" Dad asked. He didn't sound quite as snappish as he had a minute earlier.

"Lunch."

The room was very still. He looked at my mother and nodded.

"All right," Mama said. "Tomorrow I'll send a note asking that you be excused during your lunch hour. But it's only for tomorrow. I want that understood."

"Oh, Mama . . . Dad. . . ." I hugged both of them, almost crying with relief.

"I'll be waiting outside the main entrance at school to take you to the hospital," my mother continued. "The only reason I'm willing to agree to this is because Mike is so terribly ill, Christy, but I can't ask for you to be excused every day. Your school schedule shouldn't be interrupted constantly, and after tomorrow, you'll have to be satisfied with the five-minute visits at seven until Mike is out of Intensive Care."

"That's not a negotiable decision," Dad said. "No begging in the future. Okay?"

I nodded, knowing better than to argue or plead when he and Mama spoke firmly. Besides, they had compromised on their original no, and I was sure Mike would be moved to a regular room quickly.

"One more matter," my father added. "Tomorrow you should make arrangements to ride the school bus home in the afternoons."

Transportation from school hadn't crossed my mind since Mike's accident. Back in September I had notified the bus driver who picked me up in the mornings that I wouldn't be on the bus in the afternoons, and those few minutes with Mike when he brought me home from school had become precious to us. Now everything would be different.

I was aware that Mike was seriously injured and I'd taken for granted he might be in the hospital two or three weeks before recuperating at home, but the way my mother said Mike was "terribly ill" and her hint that he would be hospitalized "a long while" gave me a jolt. Some of my first fear after New Year's Eve had disappeared, but all of a sudden I was in a panic. I dared not wonder how long "a long while" meant.

S^{ix}

At school the next day I was bombarded with questions about Mike. It seemed almost everyone had heard he had been in a bad accident New Year's Eve, and teachers as well as students wanted to know how he was and to get details of what happened.

There was a bad moment for me as I stepped off the school bus because I was determined not to look at the place where Mike usually waited, but I looked anyway and felt a wrenching pain. He should have been leaning against the corner of the building, his books and looseleaf notebook on the pavement at his feet or in his left hand, braced against his side. If the weather was cold — and it was that January morning — his coat collar would have been turned up and his black knitted cap pulled low to cover his ears. As soon as he spotted me, he always smiled.

Don't think about his not being at school — don't think about his lying in that hospital bed — don't. . . . I gave myself an order, fully aware that saying not to think about the vacant place at the corner of the school building was as futile as telling the sun to go behind a cloud.

I had a slow walk from the bus to the school door as I was stopped every few feet, and it was the same once I was inside. Yes, Mike was in Intensive Care. No, he couldn't have company. Yes, I had seen him. No, he wasn't conscious yet. The same questions were put to me over and over, and with every reply I realized how many people cared. A boy asked if Mike's car had been totaled, and I didn't know. I hadn't even wondered about the car because I was so concerned about Mike.

Jill Rogers was one of the people who stopped me and I said the same things to her that I'd told the others. She was as beautiful as ever, her coppery hair framing her heart-shaped face, and for once she wasn't smiling. There was an uncomfortable second between us until she said, "I guess I'll put my coat in my locker. When Mike feels up to chitchat, tell him I said hi and that I'll pay him a visit real soon."

Watching her walk away, I was astonished to discover I almost felt sorry for her even though I didn't like her any more than she liked me. But I was Mike's girl and allowed to see him, and she wasn't. She was merely one of a circle of his friends and acquaintances now, and regardless of her breathtaking beauty, it dawned on me I was luckier than Jill since I had Mike's love.

Mr. Brady, the principal, asked as many questions as everyone else when I handed him Mama's note. "John Nichols is an excellent doctor," he said. "Yes, Christy, you may be excused during your lunch hour today. Give Mike my best as soon as he can comprehend and tell him not to worry about making up the classes he's missing. The teachers will work with him."

After leaving Mr. Brady, I started down the corridor to the stairs. Bud Warren fell into step beside me. "How're you doing, Christy?" he asked.

The way he phrased the question was a surprise. No one else had inquired about *me*, just about Mike. I managed a quivery smile, which wasn't a smile at all. "I'm doing," I answered vaguely without an explanation. It wasn't necessary to pretend with Bud. There was as much anxiety in his face as I felt.

"Anything new from the hospital?"

I said no. That was a query I'd answered a dozen times in the last few minutes, but it sounded more sincere coming from Mike's longtime friend.

He and I reached the foot of the stairs and stopped since we would go in different directions.

"Mike's being out cold for such a long time scares me to pieces," he blurted out. "Gosh, wouldn't it be grim if Mike's body got well and his brain didn't?"

I recoiled as if he'd hit me, horror oozing through my body. "Don't you dare say that, Bud Warren!" I gasped. "Don't even think it!" My voice was so shrill that two girls passing us turned around to stare. "I didn't mean to come on so strong," I mumbled to Bud, embarrassed at my outburst although I was still trembling from what he'd said. "It — it's just that I can't bear to think of — of something like that happening to Mike. It's too terrible."

Bud's forehead turned bright pink, then pale. "I ought not to have mentioned it to you, Christy. Some of the guys have been speculating about the possibility, but I should have kept my mouth shut. I really didn't mean to upset you."

"I was already upset." I gave a sigh. "I've been upset since New Year's Eve, so you didn't start something new."

The last statement was a partial lie because I was more distraught than ever, reeling from Bud's comment about Mike's brain. I'd thought about the possibility that Mike might have lasting injuries from the accident and that he could lose the use of his left arm if it failed to heal properly, but I'd never considered his not being himself mentally.

Bud and I exchanged awkward glances, neither of us knowing what to say. With his lopsided features and protruding ears, he might have appeared comical at any other time, but not at that instant. He was suffering for Mike as much as I was. The misery showed in his eyes.

The bell rang, a signal that we had two minutes to make it to our homerooms. "See you later," I said.

"Christy —" The way he uttered my name, his voice hoarse with emotion, made me stop and look at him again. "Christy, if you ever need a ride to the hospital, call me. That's about the only thing I can think of to do for Mike."

Reaching out to him, I touched his hand and nodded. I didn't trust myself to speak.

Mama was waiting when I came out of school at twenty minutes to twelve. I'd taken my coat to the last class before lunch period so I wouldn't need to waste time returning to my locker, and Betsy, who knew I was going to the hospital, agreed to keep my books and papers until I returned.

A thermos and a small brown paper bag lay on the car seat beside my mother. "I fixed a sandwich for you and brought some hot tea since you won't have a chance to go to the cafeteria," she said. "You can start on it now and finish on the way back to school."

"Thanks, but I'll wait until after I see Mike."

It was like my mother to be thoughtful, although lunch was the last thing I could handle at the moment. I was still haunted by Bud's remark about Mike's brain not returning to normal, and I wanted to ask Mama what she thought of the possibility but didn't dare. Mentioning it somehow would make it more real.

"Have you talked to any of the Maxwells?" I inquired.

"Not this morning."

She turned the car into the hospital parking lot. We were early. Mama had made every traffic light on the green between the high school and the hospital, a rare happening.

The thin, wintry sunshine didn't warm the air and it was too cold for her to wait in the car, so she came in with me even though she couldn't visit Mike. A nurse's aide hurried to us as we stepped off the elevator on the fourth floor.

"Are you the Maxwells?" the aide asked. She was a middle-aged lady with a pleasant face.

"We're good friends, but not related," Mama replied. "My daughter —'" she gestured to me, "has been allowed to see Mike."

"Wait here," she said. "I'll get Dr. Nichols. He wanted to be notified as soon as any of Mike Maxwell's people arrive."

"Mama —" The word caught in my throat.

Dr. Nichols emerged from Intensive Care. "Come with me, Christy," he said. "I think Mike is on the verge of regaining consciousness and if it happens, he'll be disoriented and probably frightened. I want someone he knows well to be there and you'll do perfectly."

Seven

Dr. Nichols gave me instructions as we hurried to Mike's bed.

"Tell him who you are and talk to him gently and calmly, Christy. Call him by name often. He may not recognize you at first, and remember that he doesn't know he's in the hospital, so you can explain that he had an accident but don't go into a lot of details about it. That can come later. Assure him he's going to be fine. That's important because you don't want to alarm him."

My yes was a whisper.

"Don't expect any miracles," the doctor cautioned. "Mike won't be himself instantly. Today may be merely the beginning — if it happens today. If you have any success talking to him and he seems to be responding, I'll let you stay a while and then bring his family to see him a bit later. Too many people at once can confuse him before he's fully conscious. Now don't look so glum. Give him a reassuring smile."

Mike lay on his back with his head turned a little to the right, his eyes closed.

"Stand where he can see you if he opens his eyes," Dr. Nichols said. "And smile."

My facial muscles were so stiff I wasn't sure if I was smiling or not, but I tried. Going to the right side of the bed, I fought to keep my voice steady. "Mike. Mike, it's Christy. I'm here with you, Mike. If you'll open your eyes you'll see me and —"

I began to falter and vowed it wouldn't happen. "Mike," I drew a deep breath and started again. "It's Christy, Mike. There was an accident New Year's Eve when you were coming for me. You're in the hospital now, but you're going to be fine. Just fine. Mike, you —"

His eyelids twitched. If I hadn't been watching him intently, I wouldn't have noticed the slight movement, but he seemed to be trying to open his eyes.

"Keep talking, Christy," Dr. Nichols ordered. He was standing at the foot of the bed.

"Mike, everyone at school has been asking about you," I rambled on. "Not just students, either. All the teachers, too. And Mr. Brady. I didn't write down the messages they sent so I can't tell you what each individual said, but —"

That time his lids fluttered, then opened.

His eyes, as blue as always, looked straight into my face although I doubted that he saw me. His pupils were glazed and his expression was blank.

"Keep talking, Christy," Dr. Nichols said again.

"Mike, it's Christy." I went through all of it once more. "I'm here beside you and I'm wearing the red sweater you like so much. I have on your bracelet, too." I held my wrist up. "I just love this bracelet, Mike, and love the gold chain you gave me for my birthday last October. Remember how surprised I was when you turned up for dinner at my house on my birthday because I didn't know Mama had invited you? Mike, you're going to be just fine in a few days and —"

An expression came into his eyes. A faint awareness. I didn't know if I wanted it to happen so much that I was imagining a reaction that actually wasn't there, but he seemed to see *something* rather than to be just staring. Maybe he recognized me. I had no way of knowing.

"Mike, it's Christy," I repeated. "You're in the hospital, but you're going to be fine. I'm here with you."

His lips moved, half puckering to form words without being able to do it. He was struggling to come back into the real world from the deep sleep he had endured since the accident. I began to talk again, saying once more that he was in the hospital after an accident.

A sound came from him, the barest sound. I leaned closer, hovering over him. "Mike, are you trying to tell me something?" I asked.

His lips moved once more. "Christy. . . ." It was a faint, faint whisper, but I heard him say my name, and so did Dr. Nichols.

"Oh, Mike —" Relief made me weak. "Mike, everything will be fine soon."

I had to touch him for my sake as much as for his. His left shoulder and arm were in the cast and his right arm, resting on the sheet, was still strapped to the board to hold it steady because of the needles going into his veins, but the board came only as far as his palm, leaving his fingers free. I put one of my hands under those fingers and my other hand on top of them.

"Mike, I'm holding your right hand!" I was as breathless as if I'd been running. "Can you feel it? If you can, press your fingers against mine."

It didn't happen instantly. I began to chatter again, saying Bud had asked about him and so had Betsy and Gordon.

Then I felt it, the tips of Mike's fingers pushing ever so slightly against my hand. Looking over my shoulder at Dr. Nichols, I nodded. Nobody had to tell me to smile. My entire face was one big smile.

"Keep talking, Christy," the doctor said and left the cubicle.

"Mike, I feel your fingers on mine and that's wonderful. Just plain wonderful. You're in the hospital because of an automobile accident New Year's Eve, but the accident wasn't your fault. A drunk driver hit your car when you had the right of way. He was supposed to stop and didn't. If your left side feels heavy, it's because your left arm is broken and in a cast. I know all about that sensation. Remember how I broke my arm last summer? You and I didn't get to the party on New Year's Eve, Mike, but Betsy and Gordon are planning to have another party as soon as you're well and we've already been invited."

Mike's eyes were fixed on my face, and I could almost feel him digging into the back of his mind, trying to be completely awake and aware again. I knew I was repeating myself often, but I continued to talk.

Dr. Nichols returned, this time coming around the bed to stand beside me, so he was within Mike's range of vision. "Mike, I'm John Nichols, the doctor taking care of you," he said.

"He's Ralph Nichols' father," I cut in.

Mike's eyes moved from my face to the doctor's. I wasn't sure if he actually recognized Dr. Nichols, but he had to be absorbing something of what was being said. His earlier blank expression was gone.

"Mike, your parents are outside and I know you want to see them," the doctor continued. "Christy has to leave, but she'll be back later. After you've had a short visit with your family, I want you to get some rest. You won't be alone. There are nurses a few feet from your bed who will check on you often."

Dr. Nichols motioned for me to go, but first, I wanted to tell Mike good-bye. "Do whatever the doctors and nurses tell you so you'll be well soon, Mike," I said, giving his fingers a gentle squeeze. "I'll see you tonight."

His lips formed the word *Christy* although he didn't say it aloud, and his eyes followed me. He knew *I* had been with him, not just that a person was there but that it was *I*, *Christy Jamison*, and I felt like crying from happiness. Bud Warren was wrong, wrong, wrong about Mike's brain. I could scarcely wait to get in touch with Bud and tell him, knowing he'd be as elated as I was. Perhaps someday Mike and I could laugh about how frightened his friends were because he didn't regain consciousness quickly.

Standing in one spot by Mike's bed for so long made my legs feel as if they had become chunks of cement, although I would have remained in that position indefinitely if Dr. Nichols had permitted it. Mr. and Mrs. Maxwell passed me when they came into Intensive Care as I was going out. I smiled at them and said, "He's conscious," noting the immediate relief on their faces.

Mama, Uncle Eb, and Jack were seated together in a corner of the waiting room so I joined them. "He's conscious!" I repeated, the statement exploding from me. "His eyes are open and they didn't focus at first, but they do now!"

"Thank God," Uncle Eb murmured under

his breath. "We have a lot to be thankful for. Did he speak to you, Christy?"

"He said my name. Or, he tried to do it. And he recognized me. I'm sure he did. I almost talked his ears off because that's what Dr. Nichols told me to do."

"Mom and Dad are to be with him just a minute and after that, Uncle Eb and I will have a quick minute," Jack said. "Did Mike seem to be in pain?"

It surprised me that I hadn't wondered about pain. "I didn't think of that when I was with him, so he must not have been hurting," I answered. "Not hurting badly, anyway. He wasn't completely conscious, but he's going to be all right. I know he will. He —"

The words lumped in my throat and I broke the sentence off, aware of how strange I felt. It wasn't a sensation I could describe, just a general shakiness. I was standing by my mother, and my knees began to wobble. I reached out wildly into the air, when something caught my hand and I realized Jack had grabbed me and pushed me into a chair.

"Christy, what's wrong?" Mama demanded. "You're pale as a ghost! Do you feel like you're going to faint?"

I'd never fainted in my life and didn't know what the sensation was. Sitting down helped. I made an effort to smile.

"Nothing's wrong. I'm okay," I managed. "I really am, Mama. Mike is going to be all right." My voice was muffled. I wasn't shouting the good news as I'd done a few minutes previously because a reaction had set in, leaving me drained with a weird exhaustion replacing my excitement.

I must have started to appear more normal because the frown lines eased out of my mother's forehead. "Christy, when I realized you'd be with Mike for longer than the usual five minutes, I telephoned Mr. Brady and explained why you weren't at school on schedule," she said.

I checked my watch, stunned to discover I was with Mike an hour and a half.

"Do I have to go back to school this afternoon?" I asked. "I've already missed English and part of French, and my last period is a study hall so missing that won't matter. Right now I'm just — just wrung out."

She understood and we said quick goodbyes to Uncle Eb and Jack, my wobbly legs turning to spaghetti as we left the waiting room. For the first time in my life I realized that emotional fatigue can be as tiring as physical strain.

When we reached the house, Mama said, "I haven't eaten, either. Let's get a quick lunch and then you'd be smart to take a nap. I know you haven't had a normal amount of sleep since the accident."

"I'm not hungry."

"You didn't eat much breakfast, Christy. Just a swallow of juice and a third of a slice of toast. You'll have a headache by dark if you skip lunch. I'll open a can of soup for us and we can divide the sandwich I brought to school for you."

As usual, she was right about food. I didn't feel as limp after eating the cup of cream of chicken soup and nibbling my half of the sandwich. She and I sat in our customary places on opposite sides of the kitchen table, so I was facing the bay window, looking out at the mountains. The nearest range was a rich blue, as blue as Mike's eyes, with the other ranges behind it fading into softer shades. A few fluffy gray clouds were blobs in the sky.

Knowing Mike was better must have made it easier for me to say things I'd kept bottled up inside myself. "Mama, this morning at school Bud told me some of the guys don't think Mike's brain will be normal. But after seeing him at the hospital a little while ago, I'm positive they're wrong."

"I certainly hope so. Bryan and I have been troubled about Mike's mind, too."

I jerked my eyes from the mountains to her face. "You and Dad didn't think — think Mike would be himself again?" I asked roughly. "You never mentioned that to me!"

"We didn't want to give you something else to worry about."

"Mama, are you talking about the concussion?"

"The concussion is part of it. Mike had a bad blow on the skull, and the fact that it has taken so long for him to regain consciousness has concerned me. So have his internal injuries. The trauma caused by the accident apparently has been a dreadful shock to his system."

"I couldn't bear for Mike to be a —" I shuddered before uttering the word, "a vegetable."

"As Eb said, we have a great deal for which to be thankful. Mike's youth and his natural good health are in his favor. Now, what about your nap?"

I gave a twisted smile. "Dr. Nichols suggested a nap to Mike. Do all parents — and doctors — have a conspiracy about sleep and food?"

"Probably. Sleep is a great healer. As for food, I don't want you to let yourself get rundown. You're going to need a great deal of strength while Mike recuperates, Christy. Keeping his morale up may be mostly your responsibility, and you can't do it if you don't feel well. There will be times when he's discouraged and that's natural since he's accustomed to being very active."

I couldn't imagine Mike not being his normal, robust self. He was seldom sick and hadn't even had a cold during the year I'd lived in Greenview.

"How long do you think it will take for him to be completely well?" I asked.

"I don't have any idea, Christy."

"He was healthy before the accident. That should make him get well faster, shouldn't it?"

"I hope it will."

"Mama, you're holding back. Why won't you say what you really think?"

She folded her paper napkin and laid it beside her soup bowl. "The internal injuries may make Mike's recovery a drawn-out process," she said finally. "That's a fact you must accept."

"What sort of internal injuries do you mean? I thought that was under control since the internal bleeding had stopped."

When she hesitated, my heartbeats quickened. I had the feeling she was deciding how much she should tell me.

"Mama, I'm not a little girl any longer," I reminded her.

"I know. . . ."

I waited for her to say more, but she didn't. The silence was awful.

"Mike is very, very important to me, Mama," I said. "And I think I have a right to know about his injuries if you're deliberately keeping information from me. After all, today Dr. Nichols let me stay with him while he was regaining consciousness. I realize I was chosen because I was there and that if the Maxwells had come to the hospital ahead of us, Mike's mother probably would have been the one, but what I mean is that Dr. Nichols trusted me to talk to Mike. Can't you trust me with whatever you know?"

"Yes, I can, Christy. It's Mike's kidneys." She inhaled deeply. "They were severely damaged and aren't functioning properly."

"Can't the doctors take care of that?"

The panic I felt must have showed. She reached across the table and covered my hand with hers. "Yes, there are drugs and treatments," she said. "I don't know what's involved, but yesterday Dr. Nichols called in a specialist who is up on all the latest medical developments in the kidney field."

I stared through the window at a tiny cloud, whiter than the rest, which resembled a cotton ball. Watching it float over the top of a mountain gave me a moment to calm down because I didn't want my uneasiness to show. If it did, Mama might hush.

"How did you find out there's a problem with Mike's kidneys?" I asked, wondering why I hadn't been told if she knew.

"Ada Maxwell told me in the waiting room this noon."

"What's the matter with his kidneys?"

"I don't know any details, Christy, just that the kidneys were the source of the internal bleeding the night of the accident. Ada said the left kidney is worse than the right one although neither is functioning as it should. Apparently Mike's left side caught the blow when the other car hit."

"It seems to me the doctors could operate and mend whatever is damaged."

"Mike has been too ill for surgery, unless it is absolutely necessary to save his life."

"He's better now, though." I spoke defiantly, sounding as if we were debating.

"Christy, I'm not trying to paint a gloomy

picture. It's just that Mike's regaining consciousness doesn't necessarily mean his internal situation has changed, and I want you to be aware of the seriousness of his condition. You're right about your not being a little girl any longer, and I'm frank to admit that sometimes I forget you're seventeen. But right now I'm talking openly about Mike's problems — what I know of them — because you'll have to draw on every ounce of maturity you have in the immediate future. He mustn't know how critical his condition is. I don't mean you have to lie to him. If he asks you questions, answer without revealing much, or suggest that he ask Dr. Nichols. You can always say, 'I don't know.' The point is that Mike shouldn't be burdened with any bad news until he's strong enough to handle it, and by that time, he may be a great deal better."

The cloud had moved, lost in a larger cloud that was a mixture of gray and white. Bringing my eyes from the mountains to our backyard, I tried to concentrate on the wintry landscape so I wouldn't think about what my mother said about Mike's condition remaining critical. I had been sure he was much better.

From where I sat in the kitchen I had a view of part of the outcropping of big rocks that formed the stone bench at the bottom of the hill. *If only Mike and I were sitting on that bench right now. . . . If only. . . .* His arm would be around me and I'd be leaning against his shoulder. In a second he would be kissing me. . . .

Mama appeared so worried that it was easy to guess she was having second thoughts about what she told me. "I wouldn't have mentioned the kidney situation if you hadn't insisted," she sighed. "Keep all of this to yourself. Mike's parents — or Mike himself — must be the ones to make public any facts about his physical troubles that they want known, and I have an idea Mike wouldn't want even his close friends speculating about any permanent effect from these injuries."

"I'm sure he wouldn't." Mike was a private person who didn't blab his innermost thoughts. "Thanks for telling me," I added.

My exhaustion must have been greater than I realized because I slept hard for two hours. Most of the daylight was gone when I opened my eyes and the clouds were moving in, all of them now dark gray, hiding the Blue Ridge. We would have rain before midnight. Or sleet or snow. January with its short days — *ugh*, I thought, and turned on the lamp by my bed. In the surge of mellow golden light that filled my room, the scene outside my window changed to black.

There were two people I wanted to phone, Bud first, and then, Betsy. By the time I talked with both of them Dad probably would be home for dinner, and after we ate, we'd go to the hospital for the 7 P.M. visit with Mike. Thinking about that made me smile.

E^{ight}

On Sunday, two days later, I drove Mama's car to the hospital, looking forward to seeing Mike alone at noon. He and I wouldn't be completely by ourselves with so many patients, doctors, and nurses in Intensive Care, but we could talk to each other since I would be the only person paying him a visit at that time. Uncle Eb had come down with a head cold and was staying away, and Mr. and Mrs. Maxwell were on the highway to Roanoke, ninety miles away, to put Jack on a plane for Pennsylvania. Greenview was too small to rate commercial air service.

Maybe I was selfish to be happy to have Mike to myself for a few minutes, but that's how I felt. On both Friday and Saturday nights I'd shared the seven o'clock hospital visits with the Maxwells, and on Saturday I hadn't been able to see Mike at noon. Like all the other students at Greenview High, I was attending school Saturday to make up one of the days lost before Christmas.

By Saturday night Mike was completely alert. His voice remained faint from weakness and he still had the strange gray pallor, but the oxygen tube had been removed from his nose, a good sign. He told us he'd had something to eat.

"Real food?" Jack asked.

"Jell-O, apple juice, and clear soup — if you call that food," Mike answered and we laughed. His family knew as I did that Mike preferred soup to be thick with meat and vegetables so that it was practically a stew.

"But Dr. Nichols says I can have a scrambled egg tomorrow," he added.

Mike had been watching for me. As I walked into his cubicle, his greeting was, "I can't remember the last time I kissed you, Christy."

"I can," I said, smiling. "New Year's Eve afternoon when you drove me home from school." Looking deeply into his eyes, I kissed my fingertips and placed them on his mouth.

"That's okay, Christy, but not what I had in mind."

"We can't kiss while you're in Intensive Care! What if I have germs? If a doctor or nurse came in and caught us, we'd get the riot act!"

"I'll take a chance if you will." He sounded like himself. "If you have germs, don't you think I've worked up an immunity to them this past year with as many kisses as we've shared? I'm not worried. With all the antibiotics being pumped into me, I don't see how I can have even a hangnail for the next ten years, much less an honest-to-goodness germ. Are you scared to kiss me?"

I smiled my no. Leaning over the bed, I kissed him gently on the lips, longing to hold my mouth against his forever. I made myself pull back, then kissed him again.

"While I was coming to the hospital I thought about lots of stuff to tell you," I said. "And now my mind's gone blank. That's what your kisses do to me."

"Want to hear my news? Tomorrow I'm to tell Intensive Care good-bye and go to a room, and that means I don't have to live for these five-minute visits any longer."

"Mike, that's wonderful! Just plain wonderful!"

"Will you come straight from school to see me tomorrow?"

"You know I will. I can't wait. How long will the hospital allow me to stay?"

"Forever."

I beamed at him. That was the sort of reply he would have made before he was hurt. It was proof to me that his brain functioned normally and that his personality was unchanged, although I didn't need proof. I *knew*.

Moving my hand across his right cheek, I felt the smoothness of that side of his face.

On the other side, below the bandage, whiskers showed through the scabs on his chin.

"Did you shave yourself?" I asked.

"Are you kidding? They won't even let me sit up or feed myself. A nurse shaved me this morning. Jenny Allen. She's the one with the dimples."

"You're definitely getting better if you've noticed the cute nurses," I teased.

"Most of them are nice, but Jenny is the best-looking one. Can you believe she used a straight razor? My grandfather used to shave with one of those, but I wouldn't dare try it for fear of cutting my throat. Jenny said every nurse has to know how to shave a man patient and that she practiced on her boyfriend. He's the one who taught her to use a straight razor rather than a safety one. That struck me as funny so I asked her if they were still dating, and she said yes. They're engaged, and she claimed she only nicked him twice when she was learning."

Mike and I smiled at each other again and I fitted my fingers around his right hand. I decided to talk in order to force him to be quiet. His voice, which was strong when I arrived, seemed to be growing thin.

"Guess what I did last night," I said, and before he had a chance to reply, I told him about going to the movies with Betsy and Gordon. "Betsy phoned after I came home from seeing you last night. At first, I refused, but she insisted and she didn't have to do much urging. I wasn't looking forward to Saturday night without you, Mike, but I hated to camp on their date."

"I'm glad you went. Tell them I said thanks for including you. I don't want you staying home every sec while I'm in the hospital."

"It would have been more fun if you'd been there, Mike."

"Did you say yesterday was Saturday? I've really lost track of time."

"That will change once you're in a room with a window. Day and night are the same in Intensive Care with no view of outside and the lights on constantly."

There was a question I wanted to ask him and was almost afraid of doing it, but I couldn't stop myself. Clearing my throat, I took the plunge and said, "Mike, do you hurt?"

"Yeah." His reply came so quickly it startled me.

"A lot?"

"Not too much right this second, but most of the time it seems like a lot. One of the nurses gave me a shot for pain half an hour before you came in and that took care of the hurting for the time being."

"If you don't have the shot, what hurts? What part of your body?"

"All over. My left arm and shoulder give me a fit, and the middle of my back is so tender I go bananas if one of the doctors or nurses touches it. If you want an honest answer, I can't tell you of any place that doesn't hurt when the shot wears off and I'm waiting for the next one."

Although I didn't mention it, the pain in his back might come from his kidneys since that's where they are located. I'd looked up kidneys in an encyclopedia in the school library to find out more information about them after the discussion with Mama.

"It breaks my heart to think about your having to suffer, Mike." I tightened my hold on his hand.

"Don't worry for fear I'll end up an addict. I asked Dr. Nichols about that, and he promised me he wouldn't let it happen. He said he'll taper off on the potency of the shots until I don't need them at all, but you'd better believe they are a lifesaver now. I don't think I could stand the pain indefinitely without them."

Jenny, the nurse with the dimples, came into the cubicle to say I should go.

"Please don't make Christy leave yet," Mike begged. "She's my girl and —"

"You don't say," Jenny interrupted him and laughed. "I'd never have guessed."

She was teasing, which made Mike grin, and I smiled, too, conscious that I was blushing. My face always turned rosy when a personal statement was made about me in my hearing.

"Sorry, Mike," the nurse went on. "But I have my orders. I gave you two some extra time today, but I can't stretch it indefinitely."

She stood just outside the cubicle to be sure I left. With Jenny there, I didn't have the nerve to kiss Mike good-bye on the mouth, so I lifted his right hand to my lips and kissed his fingers. "See you tonight," I whispered.

"And tomorrow, Christy. Tomorrow after school most of all. I never thought I would look forward to a Monday, but I do."

With so many fears since Mike's accident, it was heaven not to be as worried as I was earlier, but strangely enough, when I left Intensive Care I was fighting a sense of loneliness. Sundays were always special for Mike and me, even though we didn't necessarily go places or do exciting things. Some of the best times had been just the two of us spending long summer Sunday afternoons talking on the stone bench in the backyard, and autumn Sundays when we took walks in the crisp air and returned to my house to enjoy an open fire in the den.

Now he was in the hospital and I was going home alone, and the hours seemed endless until 7 P.M. when I'd see him again.

"Christy."

A voice behind me spoke my name as I waited on the fourth floor for the elevator. Turning, I was face to face with the man who had been on duty at the emergency entrance the night Mike was admitted to the hospital. I knew he was David Webster because of the name tag pinned to his white coat, and he and I had said hello in the corridor several times since then, although it surprised me that he knew my name.

"I heard the good news that Mike Maxwell will be moved from Intensive Care tomorrow," he said. "That's great."

"I think it's great too," I replied. "He's much, much better."

The elevator arrived and was crowded. We managed to get on but didn't talk until we reached the first floor. I was about to tell him good-bye when he said, "Christy, this is my break and I'm heading for the snack bar. How about coming along and having a Coke?"

To my amazement, I didn't hesitate. He seemed friendly, and I wasn't in the mood to be by myself. More importantly, there were questions I wanted to ask about Mike.

The snack bar was located off the main hospital lobby, a square room with vending machines placed around three walls. Chairs and tables filled the center. I took a seat while he dropped coins into two machines, buying Cokes from one and a bag of potato chips from the other.

He was nice looking although not as handsome as Mike. His light brown hair had a hint of red, and his eyes were dark brown. He was tall, with a chunky body and a hard-muscled look. As to his age, I wasn't sure. He didn't appear as old as I had assumed New Year's Eve, and now I decided he wasn't any older than Lee Carlyle whose father owned the gift shop where I worked before Christmas. Lee was twenty-one.

A little of my former shyness surfaced as David Webster rejoined me at the table and I struggled to come up with a remark that would get a conversation started between us. Just to be saying something, I asked if he had known Mike a long time.

"As a matter of fact, I don't know Mike at all," he answered. "I'm from Roanoke, not from Greenview, and I've only been working here at the Greenview Hospital since the week before Christmas. I saw Mike the night he was hurt when the ambulance crew brought him to Emergency, but I've kept up with his condition since then. Practically everyone working in the hospital has."

"If you're not from this town and don't know Mike, how did you know my name?" I blurted out.

"Asked Jack Maxwell who you were a couple of days ago."

"Then you're a friend of Jack's?" There was a compulsion in me to find out.

"Nope." His mouth curved into a wide smile. "I've only seen Jack Maxwell these past few days when he waited to visit his brother."

I was puzzled and, for a moment, speechless. It seemed rude to pump him with questions, but he appeared to be enjoying my queries and it also appeared he wasn't going to offer more information voluntarily.

"You've just fooled me, Christy," he said.

"I thought you'd ask why I wanted to find out who you are."

I laughed. "My curiosity is giving me fits. Okay, I'll ask. Why did you try to get my name from Jack?"

"Because I hoped your last name was Maxwell."

"You hoped *what?*" My eyebrows moved halfway up my forehead, and I gave him a long, quizzical stare.

"You see, Christy, I hoped that you were Mike's and Jack's sister."

"What do you mean? You're not making sense."

"I'm making darn good sense. If you had been their sister, I planned to ask you for a date as soon as Mike was better. I didn't mention that angle to Jack, but he's not so dumb he didn't catch on, and he wised me up in no uncertain terms. Said you're not available because you and Mike are an established twosome. I haven't had to wonder if he was right because I've seen you visiting Mike with his family, and you'd never have been permitted inside Intensive Care otherwise."

For the second time in less than an hour my face was hot enough to let me know I must be blushing. I was saved from having to think up a comment because he began speaking.

"How long have you and Mike been dating?" he asked.

"Since last spring."

"That long, huh? Mike's a lucky fellow even if he is smashed up."

"I'm the lucky one, David. Mike is a marvelous person, and I hope you have a chance to get to know him." I turned my Coke can around several times, leaving wet circles on the tabletop. "Mike will be all right, won't he?"

David's grin immediately changed to a serious expression. "Are you asking my opinion, Christy? I'm not a doctor. I'm not qualified to say."

"But I thought — your white coat and everything — I thought you were an intern."

"Thanks for the vote of confidence, but you're giving me more credit than I'm due. I'm not even in medical school yet. That won't come until fall. For now, I'm working at this hospital to fill the time between finishing college last December and next fall when I'll begin anatomy and all those other subjects that send first-year med students into orbit. As for the white coat, that's a hospital rule. All employees who work with patients are required to wear white coats over their clothes unless they're in uniform like nurses or in operating room greens. Except doctors making rounds, of course. They can wear business suits."

"What sort of work do you do?"

"Two nights a week I'm in the Emergency Department, which is mostly paperwork, checking patients in since I haven't had the training to do anything medical. I help in the lab, and that's one assignment I'm qualified to handle as chemistry and biology were my college majors. The rest of the time it's shuffling bedpans on the men's surgical floor and doing things like moving patients who can't move themselves. I suppose this is a good means of finding out if I still want to be a doctor. And I do."

"Where did you go to college?"

"Virginia Tech. That's Virginia Polytechnic Institute and State University in Blacksburg, otherwise known as VPI or Virginia Tech." He said it with a proud flourish.

"That's where Mike hopes to go in September. He's waiting to find out if he's been accepted there. It will kill him if VPI turns him down." My voice wavered. "I'm awfully afraid if Mike is sick a long time and can't study, he won't graduate in June."

"It wouldn't be the end of the world if that should happen, Christy. He can always go to summer school and make up the courses he needs. That would mean he'd have to forego a cap and gown and marching to 'Pomp and Circumstance' in the June commencement procession, but his diploma will be just as valid. I know what I'm talking about because I finished my undergraduate work at VPI the end of the fall quarter in the middle of December. What about you? Have you set your sights on college for the fall?"

Nodding, I held up both hands with my fingers crossed. "Like Mike, I'm waiting to see where I'm accepted, and I have three applications out. Mike and I probably won't know anything until March or April. David, did you say you won't enter med school until fall? This is only January and that's months from now."

"Don't I know it! And to think I went to school at Virginia Tech two summers in addition to the regular terms to rush to graduate in three years instead of four with the hope of beginning med school in a hurry. No such luck despite the big plans, but I suppose I ought to be thankful I got in at all. There are dozens of applicants for each opening and that's not only true in this state, but everywhere."

"Do you know which med school?"

"The University of Virginia."

The University of Virginia was located in Charlottesville, about seventy-five miles from Greenview. I had discovered soon after moving south that people in Virginia referred to it as "Mr. Jefferson's University" since it was founded by Thomas Jefferson.

"I've already been assured of acceptance," David went on, "but there wasn't an opening until the fall class — it's August, actually, not September. The dean suggested that I spend the time until then working in a hospital and he told me to apply here, that Greenview has an excellent hospital despite being small. So, here I am."

"Do you have friends in town?"

"Just the people working in the hospital

that I've met since I came to Greenview. One of the nurses told me about a vacant efficiency on Harrison Street, so I'm living nearby. It isn't the greatest, but I'm not there much since I'm putting in all the overtime possible. The more I can earn and save, the less I'll have to borrow or ask my father to provide in the next four years."

"An efficiency implies a kitchen, David. How are you with the pots and pans?"

"Don't ask." He grinned at me. "When I get past eggs and hamburgers, I'm in left field. It's probably lucky I'm not a gourmet cook because my 'kitchen' consists of a hot plate and the world's smallest refrigerator, but that's no big deal as I can eat in the hospital cafeteria at a discount when I'm at work. Speaking of work," his eyes went to the electric clock on the wall opposite our table, "I hate to break this up and shove off, but I'm due in the lab in exactly four minutes. Maybe we can do this again sometime."

It was easy to return his smile. "Thanks for the Coke and the good conversation, David. Look in on Mike if you have a chance."

"Will do." He gulped the last swallow of his drink, tossed both our Coke cans and the empty potato chip bag into a plastic litter barrel, and strode off at a fast pace.

I buttoned my coat to my chin and went home.

N^{ine}

Monday was a time of disappointments.
Maybe I expected too much and should have
known there was a chance things wouldn't
turn out the way I wanted, but I was so eager
for the long, long visit with Mike that I
couldn't think of much else.

Nothing happened as I had anticipated.
Nothing.

On Sunday night Mr. Maxwell asked permission from the nursing supervisor for
Mama and Dad to speak to Mike since Uncle
Eb, who still had a cold, wouldn't be coming
to the hospital, and Jack had left town. I
would have had to be blind not to notice the
shocked expressions on my parents' faces
when they entered the cubicle in Intensive
Care. They hadn't seen Mike since the day
after the accident when he was unconscious.

While I had become accustomed to his gaunt-
ness and gray-white pallor as well as the
bruised flesh surrounding the bandage on the
left side of his forehead and cheek, they
were stunned. My mother gave a tiny gasp,
and Dad's jaws became rigid. The good response was from Mike. He was very pleased
to see them.

Following the brief visit, we left the hospital with the Maxwells, all of us crossing
the parking lot together and pausing beside
their car to chat for a few minutes. The stars
were uncommonly brilliant in the black sky
and I looked up, thankful Mike soon would
be in a room with a window. He loved to
study stars and knew many of the constella-
tions. If he should be wakeful at night, maybe
watching the heavens from his hospital bed
would help him pass the time.

"Christy," Mrs. Maxwell addressed me,
"please don't tell anyone at school tomorrow
that Mike is being transferred from Intensive Care, because Dr. Nichols doesn't want
him to have much company yet. Mike is anxious to see his friends, but talking can be
exhausting for a sick person. A parade of people coming and going in his room will be too
much, so if you're asked about him tomorrow,
say he's improving and don't give details."

I said I would, and her instructions made
sense, although Mike was going to be upset
at not seeing Bud and Gordon during the
next day or two. He'd mentioned Bud to me
several times, and I had tried to phone Bud

earlier that Sunday after my midday visit to the hospital. No one had answered at the Warren house so I was planning to try to call Bud again before bedtime, an idea I vetoed after Mrs. Maxwell's remarks.

But Mike and I can be together all afternoon tomorrow, I thought silently, and smiled to myself in the starlit darkness.

The first disappointment Monday came at breakfast when I told Mama I wouldn't come home from school on the bus after classes, but would go straight to the hospital.

"If I do that, I'll see Mike more quickly than if I rode all the way here to get your car and then had to drive into town and find a parking place," I went on. "Will you or Dad come for me later?"

I didn't think that request would make waves, but it did. Mama carefully set her coffee cup in the saucer and gave me one of her let's-think-about-this looks.

"What do you mean by 'later'?" she asked.

"I'll have to play it by ear today. Maybe I'll eat some dinner tonight in the hospital cafeteria and go back to Mike's room and stay until the end of visiting hou —"

"No!" she and Dad interrupted me, speaking simultaneously.

"I'll stop by the hospital for you on my way home from work this afternoon, Christy," Dad said. "I leave the plant at five and will be at the hospital around five-fifteen. You be waiting in the lobby near the front windows so you can see me coming and I won't have to park."

"Dad, that doesn't give me much time with Mike."

"You get out of school at three and you should certainly be able to walk to the hospital in less than twenty minutes," he said. "Even if you're as late as three-thirty getting there, you'll still have an hour and a half with Mike, and that should be plenty."

The little pulse in his temple was throbbing, a sure sign that he was annoyed. Monday morning wasn't a good time for a discussion, but I hadn't thought about transportation Sunday night.

"I think an hour and a half is much too long for you to be at the hospital today," my mother said. "You heard Ada Maxwell last night. She made it plain that company will tax Mike's strength until he's better."

"But *I'm* not company." My mouth felt dry. "Mrs. Maxwell didn't mean *me*. Mike is counting on me and —"

Without waiting for me to finish the sentence, Mama broke in to tell me to get my coat, that I would miss the bus if I didn't hurry.

Mama was right, as the bus was in sight when I reached the bottom of our hill. My parents' lack of understanding made me furious, a feeling that persisted until midafternoon when I was actually on my way to the hospital. I hadn't wanted the breakfast-table discussion to end until Mama and Dad had seen how mistaken they were. They seemed to have developed mental blocks about my being with Mike while he was sick.

Three o'clock arrived at last, and I shot out of the school building, walking so fast I was almost running as I hurried to the hospital. It dawned on me when the elevator started to the fourth floor that I didn't know where Mike was, so it was necessary to return to the lobby. He now was in Room 319, the lady at the information desk said, and I punched the "3" button, wishing the elevator would move faster.

My elation vanished and a hollow feeling of apprehension swept over me when I found the room. Mike's name was typed on a small card fitted into a metal bracket, and below the card a sheet of white paper was taped to the door. It said:

VISITING RESTRICTED
ASK PERMISSION AT THE NURSES' STATION

I could not believe what I was seeing with my own eyes. Jerking around, I saw some desks at the far end of the hall that had to be the nurses' station.

While I now knew most of the Intensive Care nurses on sight and they recognized me, these staffers on the third floor were strangers. Two nurses were seated behind a long table, writing on charts. When I approached, they glanced up.

"I'm Christy Jamison," I said. "I'd like to visit Mike Maxwell in Room 319."

The younger nurse, a pretty blond, continued to write. The older one gave me a steady look. She had curly gray hair cut quite short and wore glasses with blue frames.

"Let's see," she answered and reached to the wall behind her chair for another chart, thumbing through the thick pile of papers clamped to a metal board. "Yes, Christy Jamison's name is here. Dr. Nichols says you may have twenty minutes with Mike either this afternoon or tonight."

"But Mike is counting on my being here much longer than that!" The words scalded my throat.

"Sorry, dear. Look for yourself." She turned the clipboard around, and I read my name with "twenty minutes — one visit today" beside it. Mike's parents, it seemed, could stay with him forty-five minutes.

"These restrictions are for the patient's well being," the nurse continued. She didn't speak unkindly, just in a firm tone. "It's now twenty-eight minutes past three and you can visit with Mike until twelve to four. Please stop here when you leave so I can put on the chart that you followed Dr. Nichols' orders."

The letdown was awful. I retraced my steps, forcing a smile as I neared Mike's door, not wanting to arrive looking as glum as I felt.

All hospital rooms have impersonal appearances and 319 was no exception. The walls were painted cream, and the furniture was made of brown metal except for an easy chair, which had a heavy wooden frame and green plastic cushions. There were two beds, one of them empty. Mike lay in the other one, close to the window.

"Christy." He said my name and attempted to smile with his bruised mouth. "I thought you'd never come."

Taking his right hand between both of mine, I leaned over to kiss him, gazing into his eyes. "I can't stay long, not as long as I want," I said and told him about the notice on his door and my conversation with the nurse.

"That's not fair," he muttered. "Maybe you can coax that nurse."

"She's not coaxable, if that's a word."

"Dr. Nichols came by this noon and said he'd see me again tonight when he makes rounds. I'll ask him to give us more time tomorrow." Mike's voice was wistful. "That won't help today, though."

"How do you feel, Mike?"

"Not the greatest. Let's not talk about me. Tell me what's happening at school."

Nothing is completely satisfactory when you have to keep track of every second of time, and the twenty minutes with Mike were filled with tension for both of us. I tried to think of small incidents that would interest him, mentioning that the boys' basketball team had won three consecutive games and that "Nutty Nadine," which was what students called Miss Callahan, one of the English teachers, had a new dress, a rarity for her.

"How are Betsy and Gordon?" he asked.

"Fine. They're both unusually nervous over exams, but then, isn't everybody — including me. Exams seem to take on more importance when you're a senior."

I wished instantly I hadn't referred to examinations or made the comment about being seniors. Mike looked startled.

"Gosh, I'd forgotten about exams," he said. "When do they start? I seem to have lost all track of time."

"Monday, but don't worry. Mr. Brady told me the teachers will help you as soon as you feel up to studying."

"I wonder how long that will be. The wreck must have scrambled my brains. I don't think I could concentrate on studying right now."

"You concentrate on getting well."

"How is Bud, Christy?"

"Fine. Eager to see you. Everybody asks about you every day. The teachers, too. I should mimeograph a bulletin each morning and sell copies. I'd be a millionaire in no time."

I was trying to joke and didn't succeed very well. The twenty minutes passed too quickly. I put on my coat and gathered up my schoolbooks.

"Don't forget to ask Dr. Nichols if I can stay longer in the future," I said and kissed him good-bye.

"I won't, Christy. I won't even let him move from the door to the bed before I throw that question at him."

The nurse with curly gray hair and blue-rimmed glasses gave me an approving nod when I told her I was going. Maybe I'd scored a few brownie points with her by leaving on time. I hoped so for Mike's and my sakes.

Killing more than an hour in the hospital lobby waiting for Dad didn't appeal to me, so I called home from a pay phone to see if Mama would mind driving into town to pick me up. She didn't say, "I told you so," when I explained why my visit ended early, although she would have been justified. She answered that she'd be along quickly and that I should call Dad while I waited for her so he wouldn't stop at the hospital.

On Tuesday, the day after Mike was moved from Intensive Care, I rode the school bus home and drove my mother's car back into town, rationalizing that since she did most of her errands during the mornings, I wasn't depriving her of transportation. When I asked if I could count on using her car for my daily hospital visits, her "Yes, Christy" came without hesitation. I felt sure she was secretly relieved at Dr. Nichols' strict orders that saved her from having to play the heavy about limiting my time with Mike.

Mike's request to Dr. Nichols brought results. I was allowed thirty minutes in his room Tuesday instead of twenty. It wasn't a huge change, but he and I were grateful for it.

"Tomorrow I can see Bud," Mike told me, excitement in his voice. "I don't want Bud's visit to take up any of your time, Christy, and he isn't coming until six. Mom said last night she'd tell him. By the way, a fellow from the lab named David Webster came in this morning to get a blood sample from me, and he said he'd met you and Jack in the waiting room."

"He was also on duty in Emergency on New Year's Eve, but you don't remember that."

"Darn right, I don't." Mike gave a weak smile. "David seems like an okay guy. He's a VPI grad."

"He told me. He and I had Cokes together in the snack bar last Sunday. Mike, how long can Bud stay?"

"Ten whole minutes. Dr. Nichols sure is a stickler for clock-watching, isn't he?"

"If I have an extra ten minutes with you today, and maybe another ten more tomorrow or the day after that, eventually we can be together an entire afternoon."

His eyes met mine and we smiled. With his right hand he touched my cheek, his forefinger gently tracing the outline of my lips. There were times when we didn't need words, and that was one of them.

I awakened Wednesday morning after a good sleep that left me feeling better than I had in ages. Mike was improving, and I guess I was learning to accept the changes that had taken place in his and my lives since New Year's Eve.

Mike had said the accident scrambled his brains, and I didn't tell him my mind had been blocked also. But now that I was less troubled about him, I could think about school. Tuesday night I was able to buckle down to reviewing for exams. I wasn't an intellectual whiz who could make A's without any effort, but I had learned how to study and was willing to work in order to have grades better than merely passing. My first exam the following Monday morning would be math, so on Tuesday night, six days in advance, I went through the math textbook page by page, marking sections to study carefully.

When I came downstairs Wednesday morning Mama was pouring orange juice into three glasses. The bacon and toast were ready, and Dad was seated at the table. My mother, who was big on family life, had a thing about our having as many meals together as possible, and that included breakfast.

The phone rang and Dad pushed his chair back. "I'll get it," he said. Sometimes one of the foremen from the plant contacted him at that time of day.

Dad went down the short cross-hall to the den, and I heard his "Hello," followed by silence; then there was a click as he closed the den door. I didn't think twice about it, more interested in seeing pink color spread into the eastern sky behind the mountains, an indication the sun would be in view soon. The days were longer than they'd been in December and I was glad of it, something I mentioned to Mama as I served myself a spoonful of strawberry jam.

She nibbled a slice of bacon. "What in the world is keeping Bryan?" she murmured and returned the bacon to her plate. The remark was addressed to herself as much as to me. "His coffee will be stone cold."

She left the table and went to the den. My thoughts were on the upcoming math exam, and I didn't feel there was anything strange about my parents' continued absence, until I finished my meal and headed for the hall closet to get my coat. Mornings at our house normally followed such an uncompromising schedule that I could have moved through the routine with my eyes shut.

Both of them came out of the den as I opened the closet door. Mama's face was ashy and Dad looked odd, his mouth taut.

"Christy, I have some bad news," he said, and I'd never seen him more serious. "You're going to have to be a very brave girl."

My mother moved to me, slipping her arm around my waist. I couldn't imagine what Dad meant.

"What bad news?" I asked.

"That was Tom Maxwell on the phone." Dad cleared his throat. "Mike died early this morning."

Ten

Everything reeled around me, the furniture suddenly upside down and the walls closing in. *"Died? Mike?"* I seemed to be screaming and barely heard my own voice.

"I'm sorry, Christy," Mama said unsteadily. "Oh, Christy, darling."

My eyes searched their faces. I couldn't believe what they were saying.

"This can't be! Mike isn't dead!" I blurted out. "Are you playing some kind of prank? Is this a weird joke?"

"Don't you know your mother and I wouldn't joke about something like this?" Dad asked.

I knew. Of course, I knew. A knot was forming in the bottom of my stomach, pushing through my chest into my throat, choking me. The tears came in a gush. But I still couldn't believe what they said. *Not Mike . . .*

he wouldn't die ... not now. ... Maybe the day after the accident it might have been possible, but not now. He was better and was out of Intensive Care. *Better*.

The hard, racking sobs left me gasping. I don't know how long I cried. Thoughts were a jumble in my mind, all mixed up with the pain of realizing it must be true. After a while I felt a cold cloth against my eyes and for the first time was aware of sitting on the den couch with my face buried in Mama's shoulder. I had no recollection of walking from the hall into the den.

The sobs slowed and stopped. "H-he — he really is — is d-dead?" I managed. I was trembling.

"Yes, Christy." Dad, who had been standing, took a seat on the other side of me and held both my hands.

"W-When did he — did it happen?"

"About quarter to four this morning. Tom said he and Ada were called to the hospital and went immediately, but Mike died before they got there."

"But why? What made him d — ?" I broke the question off, unable to say *die* again.

"The doctors don't know for sure," Mama answered. "There will be an autopsy this morning."

I jerked my head up in horror. "You mean they'll cut him open now that he's dead?" The knot was back in my stomach, surging through my chest once more.

"Christy, any time a person dies and the

doctors don't know the specific reason for death, an autopsy is performed," Dad explained. "That's the law and it's a good law. Finding the actual reason is the only way doctors have of trying to keep the same thing from happening to another patient. I'm sure Mike wouldn't object if he knew. I've never known any youngster more willing to help people than Mike Maxwell. He went out of his way to do favors, and he would be the first to say he approved of the autopsy if it would help someone else."

I looked down at my lap. Dad was still holding my hands, and my fingers clung to his.

"Did — did it hurt him a lot when — when he died?" I was afraid of the answer because I couldn't bear to think of his suffering, but I had to know.

"Tom said that apparently it happened very quickly. One of the nurses made a routine check on Mike about three-thirty this morning, and he was asleep, breathing normally. But a few minutes later the buzzer from his room sounded, and she went to him at once. He was having difficulty breathing so she gave him oxygen — there is an oxygen system built into the wall behind all the beds, so this was done instantly — and she called for the house doctor, but Mike was already unconscious. Dr. Nichols was notified and came to the hospital. All of them worked on Mike for more than an hour, but couldn't revive him."

"I can't believe. . . . Not Mike. . . ." My voice ebbed into nothingness.

A moment earlier I'd been defiant and refused to accept his death, but reality was setting in. I would never feel Mike's arms around me . . . or kiss him . . . or hear him laugh. He would never again be waiting when I stepped from the school bus, leaning against the building as he watched for me . . . we couldn't eat lunch together in the school cafeteria . . . or go to Sonny's together for hamburgers . . . or talk. There had never been enough time for all the things we wanted to say to each other. When spring came, he wouldn't plow Mama's garden as he'd done the previous April, and we could never again sit on the stone bench in the backyard, counting stars and listening to night noises in the warm summer air, his mouth nuzzling my cheek until his lips found mine.

"Oh, Mike." I spoke aloud without realizing I was doing it. The sound of my voice roused me from the wistful memories.

"I — I don't want to see him — I mean, I don't believe I can look at him . . . dead," I mumbled.

"You don't need to make any decision about that at the moment," Mama said gently. "When the time comes, just do whatever is easiest for your own peace of mind."

A new thought struck me. "I can't go to school today! I can't!"

"That goes without saying, Christy." With a final squeeze, Dad pulled his hands from mine and got to his feet, telling Mama and me he needed to check by his office but would be back soon.

My mother continued to sit beside me. We heard the motor of Dad's car as he circled the house and went down the hill to the highway. How many times had Mike and I made that familiar circle? How many times had I stood at one of the bay windows watching Mike's car until it was out of sight? The questions hurt, but then, everything hurt. It even hurt me to breathe.

"Do other people know about Mike?" I asked. "Bud? Gordon and Betsy?"

"Since the Warrens live next door to the Maxwells, I'm sure Bud knows, and I expect by now that word of Mike's death has reached the high school."

"Bud will be upset. He was going to have a chance to visit Mike at six o'clock today and he'll be terribly upset. Bud thinks Mike hung up the sun, moon, and stars." *Thinks* was the word I used. I should have said *thought*. I swallowed hard, but the lump stayed in my throat. "Oh, Mama, I don't believe I can live without Mike."

"I know, Christy. I know. But you're a strong girl emotionally, and I'm sure that's one of the traits Mike admired in you. I can't tell you his death doesn't hurt, because it does, and I can't assure you that the pain will go away soon. Try to take some comfort in the fact that Mike cared as much about you as you do about him. Lots of people live their entire lives without a tenth of the love you and Mike shared."

I shivered although the den was warm. *Mike . . . Mike . . .* I said in my heart. *Why did you have to die?*

When Dad returned home later in the morning I was in my room, sitting on the window seat with my knees drawn up to my chin and my arms around my ankles. I had been looking out of the window without seeing anything beyond the glass panes. "Crazy windows," Mike always called the nine bay windows in our house, and he liked them as much as I did. One of the first times he was inside he'd paused in the kitchen, standing at the bay, and remarked that he had wondered all his life how the mountains appeared from inside the hilltop house, framed in the three sides of a bay window.

"Christy." Mama spoke from the hall. My door was open, and she and Dad came in. "Would you like to go to the Maxwells for a few minutes?"

"I don't know." It was a truthful answer.

"I think you should. All of us should."

She waited for me to say something, and when I didn't speak, she continued. "In different communities there are different customs about what friends do when a death takes place. Here in Greenview, people usually pay a call at the home. It is merely a way of letting the family know that others care."

I was still silent. I saw her exchange a glance with Dad.

"Christy," she touched my arm, "think how desolate the Maxwells would feel if nobody came near them. And especially if the girl closest to Mike — you — ignored them. You won't be by yourself. Bryan and I will be with you."

What she said made sense. Nodding, I stood up and smoothed my skirt. "I don't want to see Mike." My voice was choked. I had never seen a dead person, and if Mike looked strange, I didn't want to know it. "I'd rather remember him alive. I don't even want to see his coffin or — or anything."

"Then this is the best time for us to speak to his family," Dad said. "I'm sure Mike's body is still at the hospital."

The remainder of that day was a series of isolated events, all of them concerning Mike either directly or indirectly. I was a robot, moving mechanically, and I even tried to make my mind go blank from time to time in the hope that not thinking about anything would be less painful than dwelling on Mike's death. I didn't have much success with that.

The visit with Mr. and Mrs. Maxwell lasted no longer than fifteen minutes, but it was an eternity to me. Mrs. Warren, Bud's mother, met us at the door, and Uncle Eb came forward at once, leading Mama, Dad, and me to a glass-enclosed sun porch at the rear of the house. Mike's parents were sitting there, and

I spoke to them but had no idea what I said, or their replies.

The word *funeral* jarred me to reality. "We're planning a graveside service in the Greenview Memorial Cemetery at three o'clock tomorrow afternoon," Mike's father told us.

"The Red Cross helped us get in touch with Louis early this morning," Mrs. Maxwell added, referring to her oldest son. Her voice was calm although her eyes showed she'd been crying. "Louis is stationed at the Marine Corps base in San Diego and is scheduled to leave California Saturday for an overseas tour. That's why we decided to have the funeral as quickly as possible — to allow him to come and to return to the West Coast Friday morning to go overseas with his outfit. He's a captain in the Marine Corps, and I know he wants to leave California at the same time his men go."

"When will your sons arrive?" Dad asked.

"Louis is flying east this afternoon, and Jack is driving down from Pennsylvania and will meet Louis in Washington, D.C. The boys will come here together tonight in Jack's car. They — oh —" she caught herself. "I shouldn't call them 'boys.' Mike used to get after me about that all the time. Louis and Jack are both in their thirties, which makes them men, not boys, and Mike —" She stopped, biting down hard on her lower lip.

"Brady is going to close the high school early tomorrow to allow students to attend the services," Mr. Maxwell said.

I tried to speak and couldn't. I felt as if I might faint if I didn't get away. Maybe my face reflected the desperate emotion engulfing me because Mama pressed Mrs. Maxwell's hand and said we were leaving.

More people arrived as we stepped outside. I gulped the cold air, filling my lungs, and that must have helped as my vision cleared and the woozy sensation evaporated.

Uncle Eb walked with us to the car, his face drawn. "Just before you came, Tom received a call from John Nichols with the autopsy report," he said. "It was an embolism in the aorta. There was nothing anybody could have done."

Nothing. The word rang in my ears. I closed my eyes, but opened them quickly when Uncle Eb addressed me.

"Christy, you take care," he said. "All of us will have rough adjustments, learning to live without Mike. It's a lot of comfort to me to know how much happiness you gave him. You brought out the best in him, too."

I tried to reply and couldn't, but I nodded. Tears came into my eyes as I watched Uncle Eb return to the house. His shoulders were sagging and he appeared to have aged overnight.

"Poor man," my mother said. "He must feel he's lost a son. I understand his wife died about fifteen years ago, and they never had any children. Mike filled a big void for him."

For me, too, I thought silently.

I leaned against the car seat as Dad drove home. "What's an embolism?" I asked.

"An air bubble in a blood vessel. Sometimes it develops after surgery or injuries," Mama replied. "Or, it can happen for no obvious reason. The aorta is the big trunk artery that carries blood from the heart all over the body."

I knew about the aorta from health classes in physical ed, but I'd never heard of an embolism. "Do you mean that even if Dr. Nichols had known Mike had an embolism, there was nothing he could have done?" I asked in a muffled voice.

"Probably not, but that's a qualified answer because I'm not up on all the latest medical developments," Dad said. "I do know that when an embolism occurs near the heart or brain, death is apt to follow quickly."

The three of us were silent as we reached home. I walked between my parents as we crossed the yard, watching some scraggly brown sparrows pecking at the frozen ground. The leafless trees seemed unusually stark silhouetted against the sky.

Late in the afternoon Betsy came to see me, driving her mother's car. I was sitting on the window seat in my room and saw her turn off the highway. Hurrying downstairs I thought I had myself under control. She and I took one look at each other and both of us began to sob.

"It's so awful," she said when she could speak. "I've known Mike all my life and I can't believe this. You must feel as if your heart has been ripped right out of your body."

"I do," I admitted.

We went into the den and tried to talk about something else, always coming back to Mike. "You won't believe what Mike's death has done to everybody at school," she said. "To the seniors, especially. Most of us have been together since we were in the first grade. Mr. Brady made the announcement over the intercom this morning and added that the Maxwells didn't want people to send flowers. But the seniors had a meeting at noon and asked Mr. Brady to contact the Maxwells and find out if the class can send a spray or a blanket of flowers for the casket, and Mike's parents said yes. We're using some of the money in the class treasury to pay for it. The flowers will be yellow and white, the class colors."

"How is Bud taking it, Betsy?"

"Hard. Jill, too. Jill was at school this morning, but I think she must have cut because I didn't see her at lunch. We have the same last-period class, and she wasn't there either. Gordon has to work at the supermarket this afternoon, but he and I are going to see Mr. and Mrs. Maxwell tonight. Have you seen Mike? I mean, since he died."

I shook my head. "I don't want to see him."

"I'm not sure if I do or not. About Jill, I think she'd have liked to go steady with Mike again after she realized Vince Halloran wasn't coming back to Greenview to live, but I doubt if it would ever have happened. Mike was too wild about you to give Jill a second thought."

My conscience began to bother me as I recalled accusing Mike of going after Jill the night we quarreled, when he gave her a ride to her house. I'd apologized to him, but somehow, now that he was dead, my apology wasn't enough. I longed to say I was still sorry . . . and it was too late.

Betsy changed the subject, but a few moments later we were talking about Mike once more.

At dinner that night I went through the motions of eating because my mother expected it, taking a few bites of meat and playing with a baked potato, ignoring the salad. I noticed my parents didn't seem to have much appetite, either, although they made an effort to keep a conversation going.

Washing the dinner dishes was one of my regular chores and that Wednesday evening Mama pitched in to help, not offering but simply doing it. So few dishes and cooking utensils were dirty that we made a speedy job of it, and I tried not to think about how often Mike and I had cleaned up the kitchen when he'd eaten with us.

We joined Dad, who was reading the afternoon newspaper. Mama picked up her knitting and I thought about going upstairs and trying to study for exams, but it would have been futile since I couldn't think clearly enough to absorb anything. Besides, I didn't want to be alone. When I glanced around the room, it could have been any evening from the looks of my family — but it wasn't. I wondered if I seemed as calm on the outside as Mama and Dad appeared to me. Inside I was churning.

Everything caught up with me, and I covered my face with my hands. "It's not fair for Mike to die," I moaned. "It's just not fair."

"Lots of things in this life aren't fair," Dad replied in a quiet voice. "We have to make ourselves accept what we can't change."

"But Mike's whole life was ahead of him, and so many people cared about him. I don't understand this. Mike wasn't evil or mean or anything. Why did this have to happen to him?"

"Nobody has the answer to that, Christy. I think perhaps we human beings aren't supposed to understand everything about life and why we happen to be on this earth. Losing people we love is a terrible blow and I wish I knew some way to make Mike's death easier for you, but I don't. Time helps. That's the one thing I can tell you."

My mother rested her knitting in her lap while Dad was speaking, the long steel needles crisscrossed in the air like two miniature tent poles with the green yarn trailing into a wicker basket at her feet.

"After a time you'll be able to think about all the fun you and Mike had together and not about the sorrow of his death," she said. "That won't happen today or tomorrow, but it will come eventually. Believe me, I know."

"How do you know, Mama?"

"You don't remember when my parents died because you were just eight months old, Christy; but they died within five weeks of each other, and I experienced a dreadful feeling of resentment and loss. Then I went through the same thing again when my brother was killed in Vietnam. At first, I had a frightening sense of separation from them and I was bitter, especially bitter about my brother because, like Mike, he was young. That bitterness is gone now, though. I still miss them and always will, but I don't feel apart from them as I did at first."

The wind was blowing, rattling shutters on our house, knocking tree branches. I suppose my parents were waiting for me to reply, and I couldn't. The only feeling in me was the ache of missing Mike.

After a while my mother began to knit once more, and Dad wrote a word in the crossword puzzle. I opened a magazine, turning the pages and pretending to look at the pictures. My parents were trying to help me and I was grateful for their love and understanding, but nothing could stop the pain of facing the future without Mike. Blinking furiously, I tried to make the tears go away so I wouldn't break down again.

Eleven

It was Mike's favorite kind of day, cold but not raw, the sunshine bright, the air so clear that all five ranges of the Blue Ridge Mountains were showing across the distant horizon.

The cemetery was on the outskirts of Greenview in the opposite direction from where we lived, a large area enclosed in a low wall with the separate family plots in neat rows divided by paths. The entrance was through a rounded stone arch, and I didn't look to the left or the right as Mama, Dad, and I left the car and walked up the shallow hill to the Maxwell plot. Ahead of us, a throng of people had gathered, some of them silent, others talking in whispers or hushed voices, all of them standing back respectfully from the gray coffin that rested on a steel frame.

Seeing the coffin made me catch my breath. The hole in the ground waiting to receive it and the pile of dirt to one side were covered with artificial grass so green it seemed out of place amid the dry, wintry vegetation on either side. Mike couldn't be in that coffin, I told myself. Not my Mike. All of this was a nightmare and I'd wake up soon and Mike would telephone from the service station to tell me what time to expect him at my house after dinner. . . .

Shuddering, I realized I was trying not to believe the truth. That gray coffin held Mike's body. I couldn't pretend it didn't. There would be no more phone calls from him, no more lovely times together.

Bud Warren, his head ducked so that he seemed to be scrutinizing his feet, stood between his parents just as I was standing between Mama and Dad. Jill was with Carl Browning, her bright hair tucked under a dark green tam, which matched her green coat, and for once she wasn't beautiful because her eyes were swollen enough to let me know she'd been crying. My eyes probably looked the same. Betsy and Gordon were together, holding hands. Mr. and Mrs. Collins, Betsy's parents, were behind them while the Sagers, Gordon's family, were next to Mr. Brady, the high school principal.

At three o'clock a long black car, which I recognized as the property of the funeral home, arrived with Mr. and Mrs. Maxwell and Uncle Eb on the backseat. Louis and

Jack occupied the two jump seats, and the Reverend Mr. Randolph, the minister who would conduct the funeral, sat in front with the driver.

I gave Mike's family a quick glance and immediately averted my eyes as they took their places beside the grave, thankful Jack had brought Louis to my house that morning so my introduction to him didn't have to be at the funeral. Jack had phoned around ten to know if it was all right to come, saying, "Louis would like to meet you, Christy, since you meant so much to Mike. He and I will leave Greenview early tomorrow, and if we don't see you now, I'm afraid there won't be a chance later."

Louis, the oldest of the three brothers, bore a family resemblance to Mike and Jack with the same lean body and brown hair, his hair cut short in military style. All the Maxwell men had intensely blue eyes. Even though Mike's brothers didn't stay long at my house, it was an awkward few minutes and none of us had much to say. I knew they were thinking of Mike just as I was.

The funeral started. Mr. Randolph opened a leather-covered prayer book and began to read: "I am the resurrection and the life, saith the Lord. . . ."

Almost in a trance, I heard him continue: "We brought nothing into this world and it is certain we can carry nothing out. The Lord gave and the Lord hath taken. . . ." Something in me said, *Don't listen — don't listen*

— *don't listen,* as if that would make it less real. But I couldn't help listening as Mr. Randolph began reciting the hundred and twenty-first psalm: "I will lift up mine eyes unto the hills from whence cometh my help. . . ." The mountains had never looked more blue. Mike thought those mountains were beautiful and he often told me he couldn't imagine living in a flat area.

The psalm ended, and Mr. Randolph began another prayer. I studied the flowers that covered the top of the coffin, yellow and white blooms from the senior class of Greenview High. The long, spiky yellow gladoli formed a frame for white chrysanthemums, daisies, yellow roses, and white lilies. Mike would have liked them. He never failed to admire the flowers in my mother's garden.

It was over at last. Mr. Randolph said, "Amen," and turned to the Maxwell family, extending his hand. The congregation stirred, no longer silent and still. A few low voices could be heard. Some of the people went forward toward Mr. and Mrs. Maxwell while others walked down the hill.

Dad tugged at my arm. "Would you like to wait and speak to anyone, Christy?" he asked.

I shook my head, not trusting myself to answer. I wanted to go home.

Twelve

I didn't plan to go to school on the Friday and Saturday after Mike's funeral. But my parents insisted that I go, and later I was glad they had. Mama brought up the subject Thursday night. The TV was on and maybe she and Dad were enjoying the program, although I was lost in my own thoughts.

She mentioned school while a commercial advertised laundry detergent. "But I'm not ready to go back to school yet," I protested. "Besides, these last two days before exams won't be for learning. Most of the teachers will review or turn the class periods into study halls, and I can do my own studying at home."

"The sooner you get back into a regular routine, the better it will be for you," Dad commented.

"I can get into that routine Monday."

Panic made my voice high. "I'll go to pieces if anyone mentions Mike, and somebody will. I'm sure that's going to happen."

"When it does, just say, 'Thank you for your sympathy,' and change the subject," Mama said. "The other person will get the message that you don't care to discuss it."

"My mind will go blank. I won't be able to change the subject." My hands were icy cold in my lap at the thought of the ordeal of school. "Mama, I'll cry. I know I will." I was almost crying at the moment just worrying about it.

"The first day back will be the first day whether it's tomorrow or next Monday or a month from now, and putting it off won't make it any easier. Your missing school yesterday and today is understandable, but no more. As Bryan said, it's best to get the first day back over with in a hurry."

Her voice was filled with understanding, but was so firm I knew there was no point in pleading. She and Dad had made up their minds.

By noon Friday I realized I was better off at school than I would have been brooding at home.

During the morning I dreaded lunch period despite having become partially adjusted to being without Mike while he was in the hospital. Betsy motioned to me when I was in the cafeteria line, pointing to the empty chair beside her. I had a bowl of soup and a carton of milk on my tray, not sure I could manage to swallow anything, and she and the others at the table were so careful not to refer to Mike that they must have discussed it in advance. School Saturday was similar.

Saturday night was the awful time. I tried not to think about what Mike's and my friends were doing that Saturday night. Going to Sonny's, no doubt. Or to the movies. Or the new pizza restaurant. When Gordon finished working at the supermarket at nine, maybe he and Betsy would find another couple for a Monopoly game as they used to do with Mike and me. I decided that if she phoned and invited me to go someplace with her and Gordon, I'd refuse. It wasn't that I didn't want to be with them, because I did. I wanted desperately to get out of the house, but I wasn't going to camp on my friends' dates indefinitely.

After dinner Saturday evening Mama told me she and Dad planned a short visit to the Maxwells and she asked if I would like to come with them. That was the last thing I wanted.

"Not yet," I said. "I'll go to see them eventually, but not right now."

She didn't insist, and she cautioned me about bolting the door after she and Dad left, assuring me they wouldn't be gone more than an hour. I was restless. Trying to watch television, I changed channels without finding a program to hold my interest, and I couldn't concentrate on reading. After a time

I went upstairs. Without bothering to put a light on in my room, I took my familiar place on the window seat.

It wasn't completely dark in my room as the yellow glow from the hall light came through the open door. Branches on the tree outside my window were flailing, making a rustling noise, and in the distance, the rim of the rising moon glowed red-gold behind the mountains.

Tears came into my eyes and I hastily wiped them away. *I have to get myself together,* I thought. Mama and Dad would be upset if they came home and found I'd been crying, especially as they were already worried about me. They hadn't said they were, but I knew, just as I realized people at school could understand the sorrow I was feeling. But if I had a sad face indefinitely, I'd turn them off. It wouldn't be long before everyone — even my good friends — would be eager to avoid me.

Thinking and making myself do something were two separate matters. My parents had said time would help, and I hoped desperately they were right. I couldn't go through the rest of my life hurting so grimly.

At the sight of Dad's headlights, I raced down to the den and turned TV on so my parents would think I'd been there the entire time they were away.

"How are the Maxwells?" I asked.

"Doing remarkably well," Dad said. "They're courageous people. Louis telephoned them from California last night to say he'd returned safely to his base; and while we were there, they had a call from Jack. We only stayed twenty minutes, then went by Eb's apartment to see him."

"How is Uncle Eb?" Saying his name put a lump in my throat. Mr. and Mrs. Maxwell had each other, but without Mike, Uncle Eb must have felt as lonely as I did.

"He seemed glad to see us," Mama said, "and he's very fond of you, Christy. He told us to 'take good care of Mike's girl.'"

Mike's girl. The phrase warmed my heart and made me sad all at the same time.

With examinations beginning Monday, Sunday was cram time for me and I suppose it was for most of the other students at Greenview High. To add to the gloominess of studying all day long, the weather was ugly. Rain fell steadily from a sky the color of pewter, vastly different from the fair heavens the previous night when I'd watched the red-gold moon. I stepped out on the porch after lunch Sunday and came in quickly, shivering. Two or three minutes in the damp cold were enough.

Few things bored me as much as reviewing. It wasn't so bad when Mike and I studied together — I sucked my breath in, knowing I must not think of Mike every second. With steely determination, I opened another textbook.

Late in the afternoon Mama called me to

the phone. I expected to find Betsy on the line and was surprised to hear a male voice say, "David Webster, Christy."

I couldn't place him. The name was familiar, but. . . . Then I realized he was the med-student-to-be who worked at the hospital.

"How are you, David?" I answered back, astonished at hearing from him. I was puzzled, too. I hadn't given him my phone number.

"I'm fine. I won't ask how you are, Christy. I've thought of you often since Mike's death. This must be hard for you to handle."

"I — I'm not — not adjusted to it," I managed shakily.

"I'm sure you're not. Not this soon. I didn't really know Mike, just saw him a couple of times in the hospital, but I liked him; and the people who knew him well said he was a super person. They consider his death a tragedy."

"David, I — I can't talk about it. I hope you understand."

"Of course. I should have known better than to mention it. Sorry."

"It's okay." I had to change the subject so I said the first thing to come into my mind. "Are you working today?"

"You bet. On duty until seven tonight. At the moment, I'm on my break. My 'well-deserved break,' to use a trite phrase. Today is one of my two-shift days, in Emergency half the night and now in the lab until quitting time."

"You'll crack up if you work, work, work and don't relax."

He laughed softly. "You sound like my mother, Christy. She worries about that, but as I told her, I don't have homework like I did in college, so the job isn't too rough. I —" He stopped and I thought he was on the verge of adding something else, but he didn't.

Talking about the hospital, which was all David and I had in common, made me relive my visits to Mike, and I dared not continue. My voice was already quivery.

"David, thanks for phoning," I said. "But I need to get back to studying. Exams begin tomorrow."

"Exams — ugh! I don't envy you. It's a relief to have a breather from them although I've bought a copy of Gray's *Anatomy*, which I understand is the med school Bible, and I'm trying to learn some of the stuff in the book in the hope of lightening my homework load for the fall. This break is almost over for me and you have to hit the books, so both of us should say good-bye. I'll talk to you again soon. You take care, Christy."

"I will. You, too. Good luck with the anatomy book. Good-bye, David."

For a long minute I stared at the phone. David Webster seemed to understand what I was suffering and he didn't question my choking at the mention of Mike's name. He and Mike could have become friends if Mike had lived.

There was always that *if*.

Thirteen

My last exam ended at noon Thursday so I had lots of time on my hands until three o'clock when I would board the bus. School buses operated on their normal schedules since some students had exams Thursday afternoon.

I hadn't been to Carlyle's Gift Shop since Christmas Eve, my final working day, and I wanted to tell Mr. Carlyle I'd like to work Saturdays beginning the first of February if he had an opening. Our makeup classes on Saturdays would be finished by then.

It was not quite a mile from Greenview High to the gift shop, which was downtown, and I was glad to be out of doors. Thinking about exams as I walked, I decided my grades might not be as good as they had been in the past because of the turmoil in me since Mike's accident and death, but I was positive I had passed. It was a nice feeling to know those examinations were over.

When I went into the shop, Mr. Carlyle, a heavy-set, balding man with a warm smile, was helping a lady who wanted mystery novels for a friend she said was laid up with two broken legs, the result of a ski trip. She finally made her purchases, and when she left, Mr. Carlyle winked at me.

"Stick around, Christy, and I might put you to work," he said.

"That's why I'm here," I answered. "To let you know I'll be available to work Saturdays after the first of the month."

He was instantly serious. "I wish I could give you a big yes this minute, but this is a slack time of year for me. I hope that will change in the spring. I'll certainly get in touch with you when it does, although for now, Mrs. Gibson can handle the gifts as well as the books most of the time. If we get lucky and have several customers at once, she sends out an SOS and I come from the office on the double. Lee works Saturdays, which takes care of help on the weekends."

"How is Lee, Mr. Carlyle?"

I had a mental picture of Mr. Carlyle's son, tall and lanky with blond hair and a smile as quick as his father's. Lee had, as he described it, "goofed off" for a couple of years after high school and now, at twenty-one, was a freshman at the nearby community college and was living with his parents. I'd come to know him at the shop when he and I had worked there before Christmas.

"Lee is going great guns," Mr. Carlyle said. "He had an excellent set of grades for the fall quarter and he seems to have settled down, which makes his mother and me extremely happy. I'll tell him you asked about him." He paused and looked at me again. "By the way, Christy, weren't you dating the Maxwell boy who died? Seems to me I recall Lee saying that. Too bad about a youngster his age having his life snuffed out."

My lips formed the word *yes*, although I couldn't utter a sound. Fortunately for me, two women came into the shop to ask for a novel on the best-seller list and I had a chance to leave.

Outside, I gulped the cold air, trying to steady myself by inhaling deeply. I knew I should be able to hear Mike mentioned or to make a simple comment about him without feeling as if I'd crumple to the ground, but my reactions hadn't improved. It had been one week to the day since Mike's funeral, the longest week of my life, and I was nearly as tense as I had been in the cemetery.

I decided to kill time by window-shopping the length of Main Street, which wasn't a large undertaking in a town as small as Greenview. If that became dull or if I felt cold, I could always go back to school and wait in the library until three o'clock. Seniors were the only students permitted to leave the school grounds after their final exams, and I must have been almost the only one to come downtown at noon as I hadn't seen others.

As if to refute that, a car horn blew and a voice called, "Christy! Christy Jamison!"

It was Bud. He had rolled down the car window and was leaning out. "Want a ride to wherever you're going?" he asked.

I got in beside him, remarking that I wasn't going anyplace in particular.

"How do you happen to have the car?" I asked. He lived too near school to ride a bus and usually he walked or, in the past, rode with Mike.

"It's Mom's car, and she's gone to Florida for a week with three women she plays bridge with all the time. Anyway, the car was just sitting in our driveway and when I asked Dad about using it, he said, 'Feel free,' which would have sent Mom into orbit if she'd heard him. I didn't need any urging so I drove to school this morning. Have you had lunch? I'm starving and can't see going to the school cafeteria today since I don't have to eat there."

I said I hadn't eaten.

"Good. Let's find some sandwiches, Christy."

Being with Bud was the way I imagined I would feel if I had a brother. He was likable and just plain nice even though, to my way of thinking, there wasn't anything romantic about him. Just as his other friends in Greenview accepted his comical looks, I did, also. I was at ease with him — at least I was until he turned a corner and pulled up to Sonny's.

My throat went dry, and suddenly it was difficult for me to breathe.

"No, Bud!" I gasped.

"No what?" He parked across the street from the soda shop and cut off the ignition.

"I can't go to Sonny's!" I sounded as frantic as I felt. "I can't!"

"What do you mean, you *can't* go there? You're acting crazy."

Blood pounded my temples. "Please understand, Bud."

"Understand what?" He seemed genuinely puzzled. It showed in his face and his voice.

I tried to speak, but instead I began to sob. I couldn't help doing it and I wasn't making loud noises, just little whimperings like a hurt animal, my hands in front of my face as if that would hide the tears.

"Christy, don't! Please don't!" he begged. "What did I do wrong? Please stop crying! Look, do you want me to see if I can find some girl to help you?"

He was so desperate I steadied myself. "I — I'm all r-right," I mumbled. "Bud, I'm sorry. It's just — just that I don't think I can go in Sonny's because it's so full of memories of Mike."

He handed me his neatly folded handkerchief, and for some reason it struck me as funny that Bud Warren, of all people, would have a clean handkerchief to give a girl who needed one.

I didn't say any of that as I wiped my eyes and blew my nose, putting the handkerchief in my purse. "I'll wash this and return it to you," I said.

"Don't bother. I have a drawer full of them at home."

"Who knows?" My voice quivered although I was trying to make light of the situation. "You never know when you'll need to pass it on to another weepy female in the future."

He wouldn't look at me but stared straight ahead through the windshield, his hands gripping the steering wheel as if the car had been in motion. "Christy, what did I do to make you cry?" he asked.

"It wasn't *you*. Honest. You didn't do or say anything. It's just that going into Sonny's will make me break down the way I did a minute ago. Sonny's is — was — a part of my relationship with Mike."

"Maybe you won't break down now. You've had your cry. But if you start, we can always leave."

"I — I don't trust myself."

Frown lines wrinkled his forehead. "Do you mean you'll never go to Sonny's again, Christy?"

I didn't know how to answer. I wasn't ready for that sort of conversation with Bud or with anyone, especially not in a car parked on a public street. We were alone, though. A few people were entering and leaving Sonny's, but I hadn't seen any students.

"Christy, if you take that attitude, you're narrowing your options. Everybody in this town goes to Sonny's and if you put the soda shop off limits, you'll cut yourself out of a bunch of fun."

I was chilled all the way to my bones. Opening my mouth, I closed it again without speaking.

"Think about another angle," he went on. "If you had died and Mike was left alive, don't you think he'd miss you as much as you miss him?"

"I hope he would. But I wouldn't want him to hurt the way I'm hurting."

"He'd hurt." Bud slapped his hands on the steering wheel. "Make no mistake about that. I'll bet you any amount he wouldn't have holed up in a corner the way you're doing, though. You're giving your friends the cold shoulder, and Mike wouldn't do that. He'd make himself go to Sonny's and figure maybe the memories would stop hurting and become good memories if he faced up to them."

My mother had told me the same thing, using different words. I made myself glance at Bud, seeing the troubled expression in his eyes.

"I guess you're right," I mumbled. "But I don't believe I can do it today. Another time I'll make myself go to Sonny's, but not now."

"Is that a promise?"

He sounded so much like Mike it gave me a start. I saw something else in his face. He was grieving for Mike just as I was, only he handled his sorrow differently, and he was trying to help me because I had been Mike's girl and he was Mike's closest friend. I remembered how Bud offered to drive me to the hospital, saying it was the only thing he could think of to do for Mike, and by being especially kind to me, he was still doing something for Mike.

"I promise," I said.

"I'll hold you to it because Mike told me several times you weren't the sort of girl to go back on a promise. Not like some other girls he and I know."

Was he referring to Jill Rogers? I wondered, not asking. He didn't explain.

"Okay." He grinned in my direction. "Strike Sonny's for the present. Where would you like to eat?"

Bud was always hungry. As for me, I was afraid I might throw up if I tried to have lunch. The tears and the talk with him had been more upsetting than I wanted to admit.

"Bud, you'll think I'm a jerk," I told him, "but I'm going to skip lunch. I'd like to go home if you don't mind driving that far out of town."

"Sure, I'll take you home. It's not that far. But I wish you'd eat first."

When I shook my head, he gave his lopsided grin and started the ignition. We talked a little, mostly about school and exams, and when we reached my house I knew he'd have come in if he were invited. I felt guilty about not offering to make him a sandwich, but I needed a little time to myself.

"Thanks, Bud. For everything," I said and meant it.

I stepped out of his car, but he didn't hurry away. The motor was running, and he put the gear into "park" without cutting off the engine.

"Several of us probably will get together tonight," he said. "Nothing big, but after all, it's the final night of the semester and with no homework for tomorrow, celebrating is in order. Want to tag along? I'll come for you."

I did want to tag along — and I didn't. That made so little sense I wasn't sure how to say it to him. If it weren't for the tearful episode in front of Sonny's, I might have answered yes at once. But standing there in the yard with Bud's eyes on me, I didn't trust myself to be with Mike's longtime friends any more than I'd have trusted myself to walk into Sonny's.

"Give me a raincheck," I told him. "I'll go next time. I promise."

"That's two promises you've made to me today, one about Sonny's and now, the other about not hibernating. Don't forget that you're not by yourself in missing Mike. Everyone else does, too."

"I won't forget. Thanks again, Bud."

He moved the gear shift from "park" to "drive." I stood where I was and watched him leave before reaching into my purse for the door key.

An unfamiliar emptiness filled our house that afternoon. Mama was usually at home when I came in from school, but I wasn't a child, afraid to be alone. On that particular day, though, after thinking I wanted to be by myself, I needed to talk to someone, and my mother could always be counted on to listen. The conversation with Bud brought aching feelings to the surface, and I'd never felt more isolated.

After taking off my coat, to be doing something — doing anything — I went to the kitchen with the idea of getting a glass of milk to serve as a makeshift lunch. When I passed the bay window and looked into the backyard, I saw my mother's car. One of her friends must have driven her to the luncheon.

The decision came instantly. It wasn't a conscious plan at first, just a subconscious idea that surged through me because of my need to be with Mike. I knew what I had to do. Quickly returning the unopened milk carton to the refrigerator, I grabbed my coat again, tore a sheet off a memo pad, and scribbled:

Mama —
    I have your car. Will be back soon.
                    Christy

The note was left propped against a vase on the hall table where she would see it. Extra sets of keys to both our automobiles stayed in a drawer in the kitchen. I found the ones to fit my mother's car and hurriedly left the house.

Fourteen

Traffic was moderate on the highway, increasing as I reached Greenview. I drove through town, made a couple of turns, and came to the cemetery entrance.

The silence surrounding me was awesome. Nobody was in sight, not a person nor another car. If it had been any season of the year except winter, birds might have been flying and chirping overhead; but nothing moved, and in the still air I heard my own ragged breathing.

I remembered walking through the stone arch the day of Mike's funeral and vaguely knew where the Maxwell plot was located, ducking my head ever so slightly as I started in that direction because for some unknown reason I didn't want to look at the rows of graves on either side. The path up the hill was well graded, an easy incline, and at the crest, one row over from where I was standing, I saw Mike's grave.

I don't know what I expected. Maybe I thought that blanket of too-green artificial grass would still be in place or that the yellow and white flowers would be there and remain fresh, knowing very well they must have withered long before a week passed. Maybe I expected to see real grass growing, lush and lovely as it would have appeared in summer.

The ground over Mike's grave was bare, the newly turned earth tamped down and smoothed as if someone had taken the back of a spade and pushed it over and over the grave until the mound was almost level with the rest of the plot. There hadn't been time for Mr. and Mrs. Maxwell to have a tombstone erected, and a small metal frame had been stuck in the dirt at one end of the mound to hold what looked like a three-by-five file card on which was typed: Michael Maxwell. The name of the funeral home was printed in block letters at the top, and the date of Mike's funeral written in ink at the bottom. The card was covered with a piece of clear plastic to protect it from the weather.

"Mike . . ." I began, whispering.

Other words would not come. I'd been positive I could talk to him if I stood by his grave, and I couldn't. I couldn't tell him how much I missed him and that I would always love him. I wanted to repeat the comments Bud and I made in the car, wanted Mike to know Uncle Eb missed him and so did his parents and my parents and our friends. And me, most of all. But the only thing I could do was stand there in the haunting silence with my throat becoming tighter and tighter.

Time meant nothing. I don't know how long I waited. After a while, I realized the sun was dipping low in the sky.

That grave with its covering of brown earth wasn't Mike, and I didn't feel any closer to him than I had in Bud's car or in my house. The strange part was that I couldn't cry. Tears might have helped, but I seemed to be carved from granite just like the tombstones on every side. Turning slowly, I trudged down the hill and walked through the arch to the car.

Mama was at home when I reached the house. She saw me and opened the back door, coming out on the steps, and my first thought was that she looked very pretty in a new dress made of a nubby material in a becoming shade of pale tan she called oatmeal. Her dark hair curled softly around her face, and the luncheon must have been enjoyable because she was smiling.

"Hello," she said. "I found your note."

She didn't ask where I'd been although I knew she was wondering. "I had an errand," I murmured. "How was the party?"

"Lovely. Lorna Erwin served a wonderful chicken dish, and all of us came home with the recipe. Did you get through your last exam without problems?"

"It wasn't as hard as I expected. Maybe I

was lucky and studied the right chapters."

We went into the house and I took a long time to hang my coat in the hall closet, averting my face from Mama. When I glanced at her at last, she was watching me. Words boiled into my mouth, words that wouldn't stay unsaid any longer.

"I went to the cemetery this afternoon!" I blurted out.

"Oh, Christy! By yourself?"

When I nodded, she said, "I would have gone with you if I'd known."

"Mama, I didn't plan to go until — until I came home today. Bud brought me from school and —"

I began to cry. The tears that hadn't appeared at the cemetery poured down my face. Mama gathered me into her arms, holding me while I sobbed out all of it, telling her what happened in front of Sonny's and how Bud thought it was awful I wouldn't go in the soda shop or join the postexam gathering and how I'd been sure going to Mike's grave would make me feel near him, and it hadn't. She didn't speak, just held me and moved one of her hands up and down my back until I stopped crying.

Finally lifting my head from her shoulder, I said, "I've messed up your new dress."

"No real damage. The material is a blend of wool and synthetics, and one good thing about these modern fabrics is that water doesn't bother them."

"Not even tears?"

"Not even tears," she answered with a gentle smile.

"Mama, I'm sorry. Sorry about what happened with Bud and now, burdening you with all of this."

"You aren't burdening me, as you put it, Christy, and don't ever feel you are when you have troubles. I know how you must feel about going to the cemetery. It gives comfort to some people, but I don't happen to be one, and I can imagine how grim this afternoon was for you."

"I don't know why I thought I could be with Mike that way. Mama, what can I do now? I can't be a zombie indefinitely and I can't stop thinking about Mike."

She waited before replying. "From what you've told me," she said after a few minutes, "Bud gave you some rather good advice."

"But if I go around Mike's friends and cry —" I looked at her desperately, hoping she had a magic solution.

"Mike's and your friends will understand and be supportive — unless it happens over and over again, Christy. The first time with a group will be hard just as your first day back at school was hard, but once it is done, it's done. It isn't too late to change your mind about tonight."

"I — I don't want to — to date."

"Telephone Bud and tell him that. But thank him for including you and say you'd like to go tonight. Bud probably doesn't want to date you, either, because to him, you're

144

still the girl Mike dated, but he has made it plain he's trying to be your friend. This has to be your decision and you must do whatever seems best to you." She got to her feet and turned toward the stairs. "Right now, I'm going to change clothes because I don't want to cook dinner in this dress."

Sitting at the kitchen table, I gazed through the bay window at the blue mountains, Mike's mountains. I wondered if I would ever stop thinking of Mike when I looked at the Blue Ridge. The sunset colors of pinks and ambers that had filled the sky earlier had changed to mauves and misty lavenders as twilight approached. Down the slope in the backyard, the corner of the stone bench was within my range of vision, disappearing into the shadows.

Mama was giving me time by myself. It struck me that if I took Bud up on his invitation, I couldn't be any more miserable than I already was, so why not go? Running into the den, I dialed his number before I lost courage.

"It's Christy," I said when he answered. "Is your offer for tonight still open? Because if it is, I'd like to go. Bud, please don't misunderstand me when I say I don't want this to be a date. I'm not ready for that. Sometime later, maybe, but not now. I just want to be with friends now." The words gushed out. I had to say all of it quickly.

He must have been surprised as his "Sure" came in a chortling gasp. "The plan is to gather at Betsy's," he added. "I'll see you around eight."

We told each other good-bye and when I put the phone down, it rang again at once. I recognized Betsy's voice.

"Where in the world have you been?" she demanded. "I looked for you at school after lunch and have tried to call your house three times since then."

"Bud brought me home and then I—" I sucked my breath in, not wanting to talk about the visit to Mike's grave. "I did errands."

"Everybody is coming to my house tonight, and I hope you'll be there, Christy. Gordon will stop for you and—"

"I just talked to Bud," I cut in. "He told me about it when he gave me a ride home and I said no, only I've changed my mind and I just told him I'll take him up on his offer."

"Bud is coming for you?" She sounded as shocked as if I'd said I would ride a camel to her house. "But Bud has—"

"Bud has what?" I asked.

"Never mind. Did he say he'll bring you?"

"Yes. Just a second before you phoned."

"Okay. I suppose he knows what he's doing."

"What do you mean, Betsy? Why the big mystery?"

"No mystery. See you tonight. Incidentally, this isn't a real party. I mean, I'm not hostess, just providing the house. The guys are bringing soft drinks, and girls are bringing whatever they want for nibblings."

"We have some brownies in the freezer. I'll bring them."

"Fine. Christy, I'm truly glad you're coming. I have to dash now. 'Bye."

There was a mystery although I couldn't imagine what it was or why she was making such a big thing out of my riding to her house with Bud. I was tempted to phone her again and try to worm it out of her, but Mama came downstairs in slacks and a sweater at that moment and headed for the kitchen.

"Christy, give me a hand," she called over her shoulder. "If you're going out, dinner shouldn't be late."

When Bud bounded up the steps of my house that night, he left his car engine running and the headlights on, and I saw the silhouette of a girl sitting on the front seat. A chill swept over me. I knew instantly about Betsy's mysterious hints. Bud had a date for the evening and I was horning in.

Jill Rogers? I swallowed hard. Mike maintained Bud had always been crazy about Jill no matter how shabbily she treated him. I didn't worry about that angle but I wasn't sure I could ride to Betsy's in the car with Mike's former girl friend.

"Bud, you didn't tell me you had a date," I chided, not moving from the porch.

"I told her we were stopping for you, and she understands. Come on."

I held back. "I'm not going to camp on your date, Bud. I'll see you another time."

"No way." His fingers closed around my wrist. "Everybody is expecting you. Kim and I aren't a big twosome or anything like that. We're just friends."

Kim Clark. Not Jill. I let my breath out slowly. Kim was the girl Bud had been drawn to at the New Year's Eve party, according to what Betsy told me. Kim was a quiet girl, pretty but not beautiful. *At least she's not Jill*, I thought.

Bud's hand still circled my wrist, propelling me toward the car, and Kim, who was in the middle of the front seat, leaned over to open the door on the passenger side. "Hi, Christy," she called as if it were the most natural thing in the world for me to make it a threesome. "Nice to see you."

When you dread a thing, sometimes actually experiencing it is so much easier than the advance fears that nothing is a problem, and that's how the evening turned out. Four couples were already at Betsy's when Kim, Bud, and I arrived, and two more couples came in later, all of us friends from school. Jill was absent and when somebody inquired about her, Betsy said, "Jill has a virus. I phoned her this afternoon and she said she'd just had a chill and was running a temperature. Said she went straight home from school after her morning exam and went to bed. She sounded awfully hoarse."

I was the "extra girl" as there wasn't a

boy without a date, and oddly enough, I didn't feel awkward. All of us sat around and talked, nibbling snacks, drinking Cokes, and giving up on the electric popcorn popper after it burned two batches. Nothing was said about Mike, and I tried not to feel nostalgic when I saw people kissing. Gordon and Betsy kissed often, and I noticed Bud held Kim's hand most of the evening. She had a sudden sparkle, that warm, inner glow that comes from knowing a boy likes you. I found myself wishing something serious would develop between Bud and Kim for both of their sakes.

Since we had school the following day, the gathering broke up before midnight. Bud drove me home first. The car radio was playing a popular song and we sang along, everything easy and natural. At my house Kim said, "I'm really glad you came with us, Christy," in a way that kept me from feeling I'd barged in on her date; and Bud walked to the house with me, standing under the porch light while I opened the door.

"Thanks for a lot of things, Bud," I said and smiled.

He gave me a salute with his right hand and hurried to the car.

I realized I was thinking about Mike without feeling desperate pain although the evening had made me wistful. *Maybe getting out with people is the answer*, I mused. Maybe time was starting to help a little. I wasn't positive, but it was a hope.

My parents were waiting up, something

they'd stopped doing after they realized they could trust Mike to bring me home safely. They were in the den reading, and both of them closed their books when I appeared.

"How was your evening?" Mama asked.

"Very pleasant." I yawned deliberately. "I guess I'll turn in."

"All of us will," Dad said with a yawn bigger than mine.

My going out must have helped them as much as it did me, because it was an indication that I was trying to resume some of my normal activities. I made a mental note to attempt to keep my grief from being a hardship on them in the future.

Something strange happened after I was in bed that night. It might have been my imagination . . . I don't know. The one thing I was sure of was that I went to sleep feeling closer to Mike than I had at any time since he died.

Snuggling under the covers, I turned on my side to face the window, seeing a dazzling display of stars in the black sky. *Mike, I went to Betsy's tonight. Went with Bud and he was dating Kim Clark, of all people. . . .* I was talking to Mike as if he were beside me, as if I could reach out and fit my hand into his. *Mike, my last exam was today.* My eyelids felt heavy, a sign sleep was coming. *Good-night, Mike, I love you,* I said in my heart, and my lips tingled as they always did when he kissed me.

Fifteen

Starting the midyear semester wasn't a big event at Greenview High since most classes were set up on a September-to-June basis and students kept the same schedules they'd had since fall.

The days slipped by quietly for me. I went to school and came home, dreading weekends although I didn't tell anybody how I felt. I suppose I was gradually becoming adjusted to missing Mike, or maybe I was learning to live with his absence since there was no choice. Nothing for me was the same as it had been when he was alive.

Our Saturday classes ended the final weekend in January, so on the following Saturday Betsy and I went shopping. Both of us had a little money to spend — hers was a Christmas gift from her grandmother in Maryland and mine was from my earnings at Carlyle's Gift

Shop. Several stores were having sales, and we were pleased with our bargains. She bought a tote bag and a quilted robe, and I found a skirt that had been reduced to half price. It was made of blue-tweed material as soft as a baby blanket and it fit me perfectly.

A few days later something I had been dreading became a reality. It happened accidentally because I drove Mama's car into town after school to return books to the public library and discovered as I headed home that the gas tank was dangerously low, the needle gauge sitting squarely on "Empty" without wiggling. My mother must have overlooked it as she was careful not to run out of gas.

For a second I actually felt panicky since we charged gas at Uncle Eb's service station and I hadn't been there since Mike's death, deliberately avoiding it because of the memories the place would arouse in me. I had only a couple of dollars in my bag, not enough to buy gasoline somewhere else, and besides, it would have seemed disloyal to Mike to go to another service station.

Steeling myself, I pulled up to the gas pumps, hoping one of the mechanics would come forward, but it was Mike's uncle who walked out of the station office. He seemed thinner, his features gaunt, and although he smiled at me and I tried to return that smile, it was obvious he was experiencing tension similar to mine. It hadn't dawned on me that our first meeting might be difficult for him, also.

"Good to see you, Christy," he said. "What can I do for you?"

Thankful he hadn't asked how I was getting along without Mike, I told him I needed gas, and just to be saying something, inquired if he was keeping busy. It was a corny remark but the best I could manage.

"Too busy to get into mischief," he replied and began cleaning the windshield while the gas tank filled.

I chattered about the weather in the hope that conversation about any topic would stop me from remembering that the first time I ever saw Mike was at the service station when he cleaned the windshield of our car. It was the previous January, the day after we moved to Greenview. My mother and I had been to the grocery store, and we had stopped at that service station simply because it was the first one we saw.

The man I now knew as Uncle Eb had filled the tank, and a boy about my age had said, "Hi, there," to me as our eyes met through the glass while he wiped the windshield. We talked a little and I discovered he attended Greenview High where I would enroll, but I was too timid to give him my name or find out his. Afterward, I hated myself for being shy and realized I wanted to see him again. The boy was Mike, of course.

Uncle Eb's voice brought me back to the present. "How are your folks?" he asked. "I hope all of you escape this virus that seems to be making the rounds in Greenview. I had it a while back and it's tough. Tom and Ada are both down with it now."

"We've been lucky so far although several students have been absent from school because of it," I said. "Tell Mr. and Mrs. Maxwell I hope they're better soon." I signed a ticket for the gas, anxious to go. "Good to see you, Uncle Eb."

As I said "Uncle Eb," I wondered if, with Mike gone, I should call him Mr. Maxwell once more, and decided against it. He would always be Mike's Uncle Eb to me. Glancing in the rearview mirror as I drove off, I knew instinctively he had dreaded seeing me following Mike's death as much as I'd dreaded seeing him. Mama was right. The first time was still the first time no matter when it happened, and I knew my next meeting with Uncle Eb would be less of a strain for both of us.

My mother came down with the virus during early February. It began as what appeared to be a cold with her eyes and nose streaming, and quickly became more than that, making her achy and miserable. I arrived home from school one afternoon to find her huddled under a blanket on the den couch with a box of tissues and a glass of orange juice in reach. She was sick so seldom that seeing her that way frightened me.

"Don't you think you should call Dr. Matthews?" I asked.

"I phoned his office this morning and the nurse said he's had it, too." She mustered a one-sided smile. "He was back at work today after having been home since Monday, and he told me he knew just how awful I feel, but he isn't writing prescriptions for whatever the bug is unless the patient is running a temperature. And I don't have a fever. I'm following his orders: juice and plenty of other liquids, aspirin or that type of over-the-counter drug, and rest. Don't come any closer to me, Christy. I certainly don't want you and Bryan to catch it."

The next day she was slightly better although a far cry from being well. When I reached home she had a grocery list waiting, so I drove into town to the supermarket where she usually shopped. It was a big store, the aisles crowded with people and displays. I was pushing my cart and consulting the list at the same time when I came face to face with David Webster.

We exchanged hellos and smiles. "You aren't wearing a white coat," I said. "This is the first time I've seen you without one."

"I do have a life apart from the hospital," he grinned. "Today I even rate the afternoon off."

"And you have to use it to buy groceries? That's a shame. Well," I glanced at his cart, which held a mesh bag of oranges, a can of shaving cream, and a six-pack of beer, "sort of groceries."

"You have a list." He sounded as though he was accusing me, but I knew he was teasing. "Does that make you a shopping pro?"

"No way. My mother made the list. I'm merely following her orders."

We laughed and fell into step, pushing our carts side by side, chatting without saying anything serious. When I couldn't find the brand of canned pears Mama specified, he located them; and when he hesitated over two types of crackers, I pointed to one and said, "Take that box. Those stay crisp longer." He commented on my buying twice as much as he did, which made me remind him there were three in my family while he ate most of his meals at the hospital.

We went through the checkout line, and he carried one of my brown paper bags along with his purchases as we left the store. "Do you need a ride home?" he asked.

"No, thanks. I have Mama's car."

"Talk about spoiling a day, Christy, you've just ruined mine."

My eyebrows went up in astonishment. "What in the world do you mean?"

"I was hoping you didn't have transportation."

"You hoped — why?"

"If you didn't, and I drove you home, we could stop on the way for coffee or Cokes or whatever."

My reaction stunned me. The half hour in

the grocery store with him had been pleasant, and I realized I was starved for companionship. I didn't hesitate.

"If that's an invitation, I accept," I said. "I'll leave my car here if you'll bring me back to the supermarket parking lot in a little while."

"Now you've made my day instead of spoiling it. Let's put your stuff in the trunk of your car and we'll be off."

He was parked near me, his automobile a six- or seven-year-old club coupe with a VPI sticker from his college days pasted on the rear window. I didn't ask where we were going, thinking more about the funny tale he was relating about his landlord, until a short time later when he stopped at Sonny's. Every nerve in my body became rigid.

"This soda shop is the best Greenview has to offer," he said. "But living here, you already know that." He glanced at me and added, "Are you all right, Christy? All of a sudden you're mighty pale."

"I — uh — I'm fine."

It was a lie. My head was spinning because I didn't want to go into Sonny's, but neither did I want to explain that the soda shop was filled with memories of Mike. Another thought twisted through my mind as if I'd become two individuals thinking along twin lines. I knew I'd have to enter the soda shop someday, and doing it with David rather than with Bud or one of Mike's other friends might be less painful.

David continued to stare at me, unasked questions in his eyes. I don't know where I found the strength, but I made myself smile.

"You're right about Sonny's," I murmured. "But how did you happen to discover it since you're new here?"

"By trying all the other eating spots and by keeping my ears open at the hospital when the staffers who are natives were gabbing. Christy, you scared me a minute ago. Are you sure you're okay?"

"Positive," I fibbed again. "I can't stay here very long. My mother will worry if dark comes and I'm not home. Let's go in."

Sonny's was just as I remembered, although there was no reason to expect changes in the weeks since I'd been there with Mike. The changes were in me, not in the soda shop.

Very few people were in Sonny's that afternoon. I glanced around quickly, not seeing any of my high school friends as David and I took seats in one of the booths just as Mike and I used to do. The familiar tabletops were marred by dozens of initials, tic-tac-toe designs, and just plain scribblings despite the fact that those tops were made of something resembling marble, which supposedly was too hard for carving. Determined people had discovered over the years that they could make grooves by exerting pressure on ballpoint pens, and the ballpoint ink left permanent marks.

David went to the counter for our Cokes,

and when he returned we found out a little about each other. I learned that his father was an accountant and his mother taught first grade. He had two younger brothers who were in high school and a sister named Julie in the seventh grade.

"Julie's a pistol," he chuckled. "Doesn't want to do a darn thing my parents tell her. Did you go through that phase, Christy?"

"Oh, sure. Doesn't everybody? Boys as well as girls, I guess."

When he asked how I happened to live in Greenview, I explained about Dad's various job transfers with his company that manufactured electric motors, and promptly turned the conversation back to David with a question about what he did for fun in college. He answered that he was a spelunker when he was a student at Virginia Tech.

"A spelunker." The word rolled around on my tongue. "I've heard the word but don't know what it means."

"A spelunker is a cave explorer, Christy. The area of southwest Virginia where Virginia Tech is located is peppered with underground limestone caverns. Some are open to the public, but most of them are privately owned. The Cave Club, which consists of trained cavers, gets permission to explore and map them."

"Trained? What kind of training?"

"You have to know what you're doing in a cave or you'll have an accident and not only hurt yourself, but the people with you. It's vital to keep in good physical condition, and you have to know how to climb and how to get down the side of a rock wall. The club gives first-aid training, too."

"Are you talking about caves with stalagmites and stalagtites? I've seen pictures of those."

"Sure am. The caves that have been opened to the public have been cleaned up and lighted, but the others are full of surprises. It's always pitch dark inside, and you wear a hard hat with a miner's light. You have to get used to steep drops, mud, and bottomless pools." He grinned at me. "And I love it."

"I don't think that's my style," I told him and shivered.

"It isn't for lots of people, Christy, but if you like it and will take precautions and are willing to get the proper training and equipment, it's great."

My thoughts returned to Mike. If he had lived and had been accepted by Virginia Tech to be a freshman in the fall, I had an idea he'd have wanted to join the Cave Club. He had a great interest in nature, and he wasn't afraid of anything. I didn't say that to David, not trusting myself to speak Mike's name. I hadn't become emotional in Sonny's and didn't want to push my luck.

It was a few minutes before five. "This is fun, but I should be going," I said.

"I don't have to report to work until eleven tonight, Christy. What about our taking in a movie or bowling or something this evening?"

Shaking my head, I was relieved to give a truthful answer. "Tonight is a school night for me, and my parents are strict about that. No going out on school nights."

We left the soda shop. I thought silently that I'd make it home before dark, not wanting to worry Mama, especially when she was sick, although she'd understand after I told her about bumping into David.

"If tonight is out, what about making plans for the weekend?" he asked. "I think I can trade duty hours with one of the other people at the hospital on Saturday or Sunday and—"

Before he finished, I refused. There was no point in making up an excuse. I told him the truth.

"David, I — I'm sorry." My voice trembled. "I — I'm just not — not up to dating. Not right now. Mike and I were. . . ." The sentence trailed off.

He said he understood, and I hoped he actually did. The expression on his face was unreadable. I wanted to say that if I were interested in dating anyone, he'd be my choice, but that seemed provocative so I remained quiet.

We didn't discuss it further. He drove from Sonny's straight to the supermarket parking lot and waited while I got into my mother's car and left.

Sixteen

Going to a valentine party by myself was too much, and I said that to Betsy, adding that it seemed weird to have festivities for Valentine's Day when the fourteenth of February was already past. We were at her house in her room, sitting at opposite ends of her bed with pillows pushed behind our backs, our legs stretched out in front of us with our toes almost touching. I'd gone home from school with her instead of riding the bus, and my father was to stop for me when he left work at five.

"You won't be by yourself at the party, Christy," she answered in the patient tone people use to explain something to child. "You'll be surrounded by friends."

"But Valentine's Day, of all times, is for people who . . ." I hesitated, "who are in love," I finished. "I appreciate the invitation

— or, rather, I will when and if it comes. But being by myself would make me more conscious than ever of not having Mike."

"I grant you that saying anything about Valentine's Day *now* is for the birds when that time has come and gone. Bud and Kim should call it a George Washington's birthday bash or something, but apparently they planned this party on the spur of the moment. It will be the first time I can remember that she's had a crowd at her house."

I didn't say anything. Betsy waited, doing a slow burn at my silence. Her forehead had a way of knotting when she was annoyed.

"Kim and Bud are having this party together and they want you there Saturday night, Christy. Want you enough to have worked out transportation for you," she said snappishly. "Bud will take you to the party and you can ride home with Gordon and me, so don't offer a bunch of excuses for why you can't — or won't — come."

Still silent, I gnawed my lower lip.

"Know what? You're becoming a hermit," she continued. "And you don't *have* to be dateless, you know. There are plenty of guys at school who'd like to date you."

"Quit kidding, Betsy."

"I'm not kidding. Several fellows have asked Gordon to sound you out about dating them. Ralph Nichols, for one. The boys didn't ask you for dates when Mike was alive because everyone knew you were Mike's girl, but now, it's different."

"I don't want to date." A long sigh came from me. *And definitely not Ralph Nichols,* I thought silently. He was nice but being with him would make me remember how his father took care of Mike in the hospital.

"You don't want to date and you don't want to go anywhere alone, so what does that leave?" She picked a wisp of lint off the bedspread and rolled it between her thumb and forefinger. "Why don't you invite someone on your own, Christy? What about Lee Carlyle? You worked with him at the gift shop long enough to know him well and even if he's older than the rest of us, that won't matter."

I shook my head, on the defensive again. "You don't understand because you still have Gordon," I murmured. "Anyhow, I haven't heard from Kim or Bud and I may not be invited. You and I probably are wasting time talking about it."

"You'll be invited. I know that for sure. Kim and Bud only cooked up this party last night, and she hasn't gotten around to contacting everybody. They phoned here first because they wanted to make sure Gordon and I would bring you home afterward. Bud was so close to Mike he's trying very hard to look after you."

The silence between us was thick enough to cut with a knife. I had the impression Betsy was disgusted with me, and I didn't want her to feel like that. Her attitude would have been different if Gordon had been the one to die, something she seemed incapable of grasping.

She reached behind her back to plump her pillow. "Christy, will you get mad if I level with you?" she asked.

I attempted to laugh, but it was a Minnie Mouse squeak. "You're putting me on the spot," I told her, hoping to hide my nervousness, not at all sure I wanted to hear whatever she was about to say. "You act as if you're ready to list my faults."

"Well," her face turned pink, "maybe one little fault. People want to help you, but no one knows how and you won't let any of us try."

"I don't know what you mean," I replied stiffly.

"Think about your friends and Mike's friends. You'd make the rest of us feel better if you warmed up a little. We're trying to help for your sake, but it's for Mike's sake, too. I realize this is a horrible time for you and I can see your not wanting to *love* any guy but Mike, but you don't have to be *in love* with a boy to go out with him."

"I know.... It's just ... just...." I didn't finish.

She appeared so troubled I knew she was truly upset. "I'm embarrassed for mentioning it, Christy," she said. "You must hate me for talking to you this way."

"I couldn't hate you if I tried. I guess I've concentrated on myself so long I haven't thought about how Mike's death affected other people." I sucked my breath in. "Being a hermit is gross, so I'll take you up on that bit about riding home with you and Gordon after the party. If Bud offers to drive me there, I'll say yes; and if he doesn't, Dad can drop me off at Kim's, and I'll still come home with you. Okay?"

"I'm so glad you're coming." She sounded relieved.

I made another of those silent promises to myself — to put my personal feelings behind me and make myself go places and do things in the future. It wouldn't be easy, but I'd do my best.

"Bud is really turned on by Kim, isn't he?" I remarked to get the conversation away from my problems.

"Is he ever!" She rolled her eyes. "I honestly think it's the first time he's ever been serious about a girl other than Jill, and it must be a new experience for him to go with somebody who treats him decently. Jill wiped her feet on him and all of us tried to tell him that, but he wouldn't listen. This is a brand new world for him. For Kim, too. I'll bet she never had half a dozen dates in her life until she and Bud discovered one another. They're so happy they positively radiate."

"Mike would get a big charge out of seeing Bud this happy."

"Yes, he would." She gave me a long look. "And he'd be awfully down if he knew how unhappy you are."

"I can't help how I feel, Betsy. I miss Mike so much I don't think I can live the rest of my life without him."

She didn't speak but she nodded, and that time I knew she understood.

The party was rechristened "February Frolics," whatever that name implied. It seems Kim had read a magazine article on parties and the woman who wrote it claimed every successful party needed a theme. Apparently I wasn't the only person who thought it was ridiculous to call it a Valentine's Day to-do after the fourteenth of the month was gone because several cracks were made about that at school away from Kim's and Bud's hearing.

I went Saturday night, and was glad I did. It wasn't different from other teenage parties in Greenview despite the so-called theme, just in a different house. The stereo was playing the entire time, and Kim's mother had gone to lots of trouble making a cake, a cheese dip, and fixing tiny miniature sandwiches that the guys wolfed down whole.

I made a point of speaking to everyone and kept a determined smile even when I was face to face with Jill who had come with Carl Browning. Jill's laughter was loud enough to be heard constantly over the various conversations. I hated to admit it to myself, but she'd never looked more beautiful, her complexion glowing and her auburn hair sparkling with gold highlights.

As planned, I rode home with Gordon and Betsy, the three of us on the front seat of Gordon's automobile with Betsy in the middle. I tried not to notice that one of her hands rested on his knee, and his arm was around her shoulders while he steered with his free hand. That was the way Mike and I often sat in the car. I closed my eyes for a moment to try to recapture the warmth of Mike's body against mine and the clean smell of him and the feather-light way he rubbed his cheek against mine when he was keeping his gaze on the traffic.

The memory was deep inside me, but I couldn't see him or touch him. Opening my eyes, I realized we were almost at my house.

In my room that night after I undressed, I picked up the framed snapshot of Mike, which was my favorite picture of him. It had been taken the previous summer in the backyard when Dad was trying out a new camera lens, and caught Mike leaning against one of the huge oak trees. Mike's fingers were in the side pockets of his jeans with his thumbs outside, resting on the blue denim. Sunshine filtered through the leafy tree branches to put dappled shadows around him, and he was smiling that wonderfully warm smile of his.

For a long time I stared at the picture before returning it to the top of my chest of drawers. "Good-night, Mike," I whispered.

Seventeen

During the week following the party at Kim's house, in spite of the promises to myself to go out more and the assurance I had given Betsy about ceasing to be a hermit, I turned down an invitation from Ralph Nichols to eat at the new pizza restaurant Saturday night. My response to Ralph wasn't curt or cold, just a no. He stopped me in the hall at school after English class on Thursday, and I thanked him, saying that I already had weekend plans.

"I'm disappointed," he said. "Maybe we can do it another time."

I nodded, and we hurried in opposite directions to our next classes. I expected a backlash from the refusal because I thought Ralph might tell Gordon who undoubtedly would pass it on to Betsy, but that didn't happen. During the remainder of Thursday and all day Friday I fought down a sense of guilt every time I saw Ralph at school, as if I'd done something terribly wrong, and that guilt may have been a factor in the way I answered David Webster Friday night.

The weekend stretched out endlessly. With nothing special planned for either Friday or Saturday night, I half wished I hadn't given Ralph such a speedy negative reply. Fighting loneliness by myself made the memories of Mike more painful. The next time I received an invitation, I'd be smart enough to accept, I decided. *If* there was a next time. The *if* made my throat feel raw. Another invitation might not come.

On Friday night I was finishing the dinner dishes when Mama came to the kitchen to tell me I had a phone call. "It's a boy but he didn't give his name and his voice isn't familiar," she said.

Ralph again? I wondered as I went to the den to answer. It couldn't be Bud or my mother would have recognized him, and I doubted if any other boy would call me unless Gordon was delivering a message for Betsy.

David was on the line and he plunged right into his speech. "I'm taking my break at work so I'll have to be quick," he said. "Would you like to ride to Charlottesville with me tomorrow? I have the day off from the hospital because I need to make arrangements about a room for the fall and to talk

170

to somebody in the med school dean's office about my schedule. It's only seventy-five miles from Greenview to Charlottesville, and we'll be back in the afternoon. You'll have to amuse yourself while I'm doing my business, but you can roam around the campus or shop or just sit in the car and read, and lunch won't be a problem. Every college town has plenty of eating places."

I hesitated even though I knew I'd enjoy being with David and that making the trip would give me something to occupy my time. But would I be disloyal to Mike if I went? The question burned into my brain.

"Christy," David's voice softened, "you'll do me a big favor if you come. I hate going alone."

That remark made the decision for me. I told him yes, surprised at the enthusiasm in my reply.

"Super, Christy," he answered with the same enthusiasm. "Is it okay if I come for you at nine in the morning? You probably like to sleep late on weekends, but I phoned Charlottesville today and the dean's office closes at one o'clock Saturday afternoons. The fellow I talked with told me he'd expect me between eleven and noon, and I want to allow plenty of time."

"Nine suits me although I can be ready earlier if you want." Remembering that he'd never been to my house, I said, "David, do you know where I live?"

"Sure do. The tall white house with all the

bay windows, the place on top of a hill a couple of miles west of town. Right?"

"Right."

"Christy, somebody told me your house has a bay window in every room."

"Right again." I smiled into the phone. "Even a bay window in the kitchen. The man who built the house in the early nineteen hundreds wanted each room to have a view of the mountains."

I was dying to ask the identity of the "somebody" who'd given him my address and the house information, but I didn't. If he had wanted to use that person's name rather than the vague "somebody," he would have done it.

Also, there were two good reasons not to prolong the conversation. The first was because he was on his break and would have to hang up shortly, and the second had to do with me. I was using the den phone with my parents a few feet away since they were in that room watching TV when David called, and I didn't like to talk to a boy with them listening. That had been true when Mike phoned. It wasn't because secret things were being said, but some of my old shyness about boys lingered from the time when I almost despaired of a boy ever noticing me, and it was hard not to feel self-conscious with an audience.

As I told David good-bye, Mama said, "I gather you have interesting plans for tomorrow."

"David Webster has to go to Charlottesville to see about his fall schedule at med school and he wanted to know if I'd like to ride with him." As I spoke, I realized I'd never before gone out of town without getting my parents' permission. "That will be all right, won't it?" I went on quickly. "You remember David, don't you? He works at the hospital."

I couldn't bring myself to identify him by saying he was on duty in Emergency the night Mike was hurt, an explanation that wasn't necessary as they said, "Yes," in unison.

They didn't toss more questions at me although David's call must have surprised them, since they didn't know he'd taken me to Sonny's the day I went to the supermarket when Mama was sick. I hadn't deliberately refrained from mentioning it, just hadn't found the proper time to do it. My mother had been asleep on the den couch when I had come from the grocery store that afternoon and I'd carried my bags to the kitchen, putting the groceries where they belonged, being careful not to make enough noise to wake her. By the time Dad had come in, I had dinner ready, and after we ate, homework assignments had to be done.

Going to Sonny's with David was a milestone to me since it was my first time there since Mike's death, and it also was such a deeply personal matter I didn't want to discuss it, not even with my mother.

Eighteen

Saturday was cold and overcast, the sort of weather I'd come to accept in the mountains in winter. Mama and I stayed at the breakfast table, killing time until nine o'clock. Dad had already gone into town because, while the plant he managed was closed on weekends, he often went to his office Saturday mornings to catch up on paperwork.

"You and David please be careful," my mother said, her eyes fixed on the dreary landscape visible through the bay window in the kitchen. "If it rains, as cold as it is, the rain may be icy, and the roads will be dangerous."

"We will," I assured her. She had a deep fear of automobile accidents, and I knew her dread had to be worse since Mike's tragedy. To change the subject, I inquired about her plans for the day.

"Not much of anything. I want to write a few letters and I think I'll make beef stew for dinner tonight. That's always good in this sort of weather. The beef is in the freezer, and I'd better get it out now so it can thaw —" The doorbell interrupted her.

I went to greet David. Tan slacks and a brown blazer showed under his raincoat. It was the first time I'd seen him dressed up, and I thought privately he should make a marvelous impression on the med school dean. It wasn't only his clothes, but his obvious intelligence and good manners.

He and I didn't say anything earth-shaking on the way to Charlottesville although we chatted and laughed. He related funny episodes about his family, and I found myself telling him about the time Mama baked an applie pie when we were having guests and didn't realize until the dessert was served that she'd taken the wrong can from the spice cabinet and used red pepper instead of cinnamon.

Halfway to Charlottesville, the rain began, a drizzle at first and suddenly a downpour that was a challenge for the windshield wipers. David slowed and turned on the headlights. Gray mist made a curtain around us.

"If you want to look on the bright side, there's one good angle to this ungodly weather," he commented. "It's so bad we aren't bothered with much traffic."

"Or with much scenery," I chimed in. It

wasn't an especially humorous remark, but both of us smiled.

The rain was still heavy when we reached the University of Virginia, water drumming on top of the car. "You'll be drenched if you try a walking tour of the campus," he said. "Stay put and we'll ride around later. I'll show you the Rotunda and some of the other famous buildings."

"Don't worry about me, David. I brought a paperback." I gestured to my purse. "Take all the time you want."

"I'll leave the car keys with you, but don't run the heater unless you turn on the motor. If you get so cold you can't stand it, brave the rain and go inside one of the buildings."

Insisting once more that I would be fine, I watched him dodge puddles on the pavement as he dashed across the street.

My paperback was assigned reading for English and definitely wasn't a fascinating story, to my way of thinking. Sitting there alone, I let my thoughts wander. I realized I'd enjoyed the drive from Greenview and while David Webster wasn't Mike, he possessed a lot of Mike's characteristics. Both of them were gentle, or they acted gentle around me; and in cautioning me about getting chilled, David was thinking of me as Mike would have done. I was independent, but it was nice to have a boy care about my comfort and safety.

David was gone about an hour. "How was it?" I asked as he opened the car door and got in beside me. Guessing his answer wasn't hard from the way he beamed.

"Couldn't have been better. The people I met were really helpful. I now have a tentative class schedule and know where I'll be living, so I feel a lot more secure."

He turned on the ignition and the heater gave a blast of icy air, immediately sending forth warmth. "What about you?" he said. "Are you frozen?"

"Not completely."

"You mean your toes haven't dropped off from the cold?"

"Why, Doctor Webster, you're already diagnosing," I teased. "And through my shoes, no less. You must have X-ray eyes or something."

We laughed. Mike and I had kidded like that and I hadn't been able to do it since his death. It was a good sensation not to be so overwhelmed with sadness that I could think of nothing except grief.

"Want some lunch?" David asked, and when I nodded, he said, "Me, too. One of the interns at Greenview Hospital went to school here and he gave me the names of a couple of places he thinks are good."

We went to a German restaurant tucked between two stores, choosing knockwurst and melted cheese sandwiches, finishing with hot apple strudel and large mugs of coffee. David was so hungry I wondered if he had skipped breakfast, and wished I'd thought to suggest that he come to my house before nine and eat with us. In the next moment I decided he might have been more nervous about the time in the dean's office than he appeared. Now that the session was over and he'd relaxed, he could enjoy food.

When we left the restaurant, he gave me my tour of the campus. A heavy rain continued to fall. "We won't see everything," he said. "Just part of the area designed by Thomas Jefferson, who was a fantastic man.

"Look to your left, Christy. That red brick building in the center, the one with the dome, is the Rotunda, and the grassy area around it with the long colonnades on either side is called the Lawn because that's what Jefferson called it."

"Are those buildings still used?"

"You bet. Admissions and the information office are in the Rotunda, and faculty members live in the two-story pavilions. Some fourth-year students — specially selected students — room below on the Lawn. There's space for fifty students, more or less, on the Lawn. It's a real honor to rate a room there, but the building has no baths and you have to go outside for a shower. I guess it means weighing inconvenience against living in a historic setting."

I said, "It's awesome to look at something over two hundred years old. Time is relative, though. If we were in Europe, a building two hundred years old might be considered practically new."

"Have you been to Monticello, Jefferson's home?" he asked.

I shook my head.

"Want to go? It's open to the public and it's near town. I haven't been there in a long time, not since I was in the fourth grade. In this state all kids study Virginia history in the fourth grade, and our school usually brought students here to visit Monticello at the end of the term. I was impressed then, and I'd like to see it through adult eyes now."

Heading east, he drove out of Charlottesville and turned the car from the highway onto a narrower road that wound up, up, up a mountain until I felt as if we were climbing to the sky. There were dense woods on either side, the trees dripping with rainwater.

"Did Mr. Jefferson live on top of a mountain?" I asked.

"Right. That's what the word *Monticello* means. Little mountain. Think of transporting everything up this mountain by mules and wagons, or riding horseback or in a stagecoach. The road was probably one big mudhole in colonial days with as much rain as we've had in the last few hours. Mr. Jefferson never finished building Monticello. He was always tearing part of the house down and redoing it."

We made the last curve, and the house was before us, similiar in style to the Rotunda with a dome and white columns against the red brick entrance. Once we were inside, I was surprised that it was so much larger than it appeared. I was fascinated by Mr. Jefferson's inventions, his alcove bed and the chaise he designed that had a built-in table for writing, and his dumbwaiter. A guide showed us the house, allowing us to return after the tour for second looks at anything we wanted to see again. I couldn't take my eyes off the handsome colonial furniture.

"Christy, it's past four o'clock," David reminded me. "We won't make it to Greenview before dark. Will your mother worry?"

"She always does. I didn't realize we'd been here so long."

"We can find a pay phone and call her. My mother worries, too."

Thanking him, I realized this was another trait of his that made me think of Mike. Thoughtfulness.

The rain ended while we were at Monticello, and the air was a little clearer when we went down the mountain and started home. Occasional glimpses of the Blue Ridge assured us the storm was over, those mountains still a misty gray rather than blue. The February twilight became an early darkness.

We covered several miles and I wasn't conscious of being silent until David said, "Are they worth the proverbial penny, or are you taking a nap?"

"Neither," I answered and laughed softly. "I was thinking about the good time I've had today."

I can't explain what I said next. The words

popped out of my mouth like tiny bullets and I wished instantly I'd kept quiet, but it was too late then.

"David, who was the 'somebody' who told you where I live and mentioned all the bay windows in my house?" I asked, speaking so fast I sounded breathless.

"Jack Maxwell."

Turning sideways on the car seat, I glued my eyes to his face. "Do you mean Mike's brother?"

"Yes, but why are you making such a big deal out of it? Is there something I don't know?"

"I was — was just curious. It's not important." It was important to me although I didn't want to admit it.

"Do you remember I told you once I hoped you were Mike's sister?"

"Yes."

"By the time Jack set me straight on that, I'd found out from him that you hadn't lived in Virginia long and that your house was one of the Greenview landmarks because of its architecture, especially those bay windows. Later I rode by but didn't have the nerve to drive up the hill and ring your doorbell."

I was dumbfounded. "Why would you need nerve to do that?"

He didn't reply instantly. The tires made a muted hum on the wet pavement, and the highway was a shiny black ribbon in front of us in the glow of the headlights. David looked straight ahead as if he'd been hypnotized by the white line, his profile a silhouette and his chin firm.

"The day I rode by was after you and I went to Sonny's," he said slowly. "I had tried to take you out and you'd made it clear you were too wrapped up in Mike, even though he was dead, to want to date, and I didn't know if you were against dating in general or just against dating me. I thought about that, thought about it heaps, and I decided if I ever wanted to get to first base with you, it wouldn't be smart for me to make a pest of myself and hound you with calls. I didn't want to give you a chance to slam your door in my face."

"David, I would never slam the door in your face!"

"Promise?" He sounded as if he was joking, but he was serious, too.

"I promise," I told him.

Turning his head, he gave me a quick glance. "If you want the truth, Christy, it took a lot of guts on my part to phone you Friday night and ask if you wanted to come with me today. I was scared silly you'd turn me down and tell me to get lost."

All of the sudden it was important for me to make David understand why I had rejected him. If darkness hadn't fallen, I might not have been able to continue talking about something as personal and as precious as my relationship with Mike. Yet, it seemed vital to tell David I hadn't merely put *him* off, but

I'd done that to everyone, girls as well as boys.

"Mike and I had something special." My voice was amazingly calm despite the way my heart pounded my ribs. "I think it was real love although I don't have any other love for a comparison because he is — was — the only boy I ever dated seriously. His death made me feel as if I'd died, too, as if part of me was gone. I'm trying to — to — What is the phrase people use? To pick up my life. Knowing you has been a wonderful help."

"Thanks, but please don't use past tense, Christy. Can't you say that knowing me *is* a wonderful help?"

Some of my tension was gone after the explanation to him, which had a cleansing effect on me, and I smiled. "You'll make a good doctor," I said. "You're careful about details."

"Thanks again, because that's a nice testimonial. But what about the past tense verb?"

"Knowing you *is* wonderful. Honest." After I spoke, I giggled. "Does using the present tense mean I'm now out of your doghouse?"

"You never were in my doghouse."

I expected him to give a light comeback and for our serious conversation to end, but when he said I was never in his doghouse, he sounded so solemn I didn't know how to answer. We were quiet briefly as we reached Greenview and drove through town. My house was a tall sentinel atop the hill with welcoming lights showing through some of the bay windows and smoke curling from the chimney.

"Christy, today has been too much fun to have it end so soon," he said. "You know I work crazy hours and I don't report to the hospital until eleven tonight, but I'm on duty until seven tomorrow morning and go back on the job at three tomorrow afternoon. I have to grab a couple of hours' sleep before eleven or I'll fall on my face about daybreak and it means I'll have to tell you good-night around eight or so tonight. But we can stop off somewhere now for dinner."

All kinds of thoughts tumbled through my mind. I was aware of wanting to see more of David and, like him, I didn't want the day to end. I was practical, though. It would be a big rush for us to go to dinner in a restaurant and besides, he was saving what he earned toward his med school expenses. He had bought my lunch and if he also paid for my dinner, which I knew he would insist on, two meals in one day, it could make a dreadful hole in his budget.

"Why don't you come in for dinner at my house?" I asked him just as I'd have done if I'd been in Mike's car. "Mama is making beef stew and that's one of her specialties. She always puts potatoes and onions and carrots in it, and has lots of brown gravy. She makes a huge amount and there will be plenty and —"

"Whoa," he cut in, grinning. "You don't have to give me the big sales pitch. I accept."

There was no reason for us to laugh as he drove up the hill, but we did.

"Christy, my next night off won't be until Friday," he said as he parked and cut off the ignition. "That's not a school night for you. What about a movie?"

"What was the crack you just made about my not needing to give you the big sales pitch? You don't have to do that for me, either. Friday is fine."

My mother must have been watching for the car because she met us at the door, a letter in her hand. She said, "Fine," when I announced that I had invited David for dinner, and she held the letter out to me. "This came today and I've been dying to open it, but it's addressed to you, Christy, so I didn't," she said. "It's from the University of Virginia. Maybe it's news about your application for next fall."

I ripped the envelope open. The letter was an acceptance for me to be a freshman. As I looked from my mother to David, I was one big smile.

"That's great!" David exclaimed. "We'll be on the same campus and can see something of each other."

Dinner was pleasant as my parents made David welcome, and conversation at the table was easy. I thought I might be too excited over the letter to think of food, and maybe a little self-conscious over sitting across from any boy but Mike with Mama and Dad there, but I wasn't. The stew was delicious, and my mother had made a salad and fixed brownies.

David didn't have time to linger. When I walked to the door with him, thanking him again for the trip, I knew instinctively that he was thinking about kissing me good-night. In one sense, I'd have liked him to do it, but in another way I wasn't ready for any kisses except Mike's and I didn't know how to put that into words.

A lamp on the hall table cast a soft, amber light around us. If I had leaned toward David even the tiniest bit or given him any indication of wanting to be kissed, he would have done it. He was using lots of willpower to refrain — I realized that.

Maybe later, David, I thought silently. *After we know one another better. . . .*

I didn't say it aloud because I couldn't, but he understood. I could read it in his eyes. He had both my hands in his and gave them a gentle squeeze.

"See you Friday. I'll phone you before then and we'll arrange a time," he whispered and was gone.

At half-past eight I wasn't ready to go to bed but I needed to be by myself. Mama and Dad were in the den. I gave them the excuse of wanting to finish the book assigned for English and went upstairs. But once I was there, that book never entered my mind.

As always, the house creaked and groaned at night, something to be expected in an old frame structure. I turned on the bedside lamp in my room, a little surprised at not experiencing the aching loneliness that had been part of me since New Year's Eve. Taking Mike's picture from the chest of drawers, I carried it to the window seat.

No stars showed and the moon was hidden, but the sky was more luminous than it had been earlier in the evening. That might mean the promise of sunshine Sunday. I hoped it did. While I was looking through the bay window, the clouds shifted, giving me a glimpse of one star. It vanished quickly, but somehow it was an omen.

I didn't need to see the picture to know how Mike looked, but I gazed at it, just the same. He leaned against the oak tree, his hands in the pockets of his jeans with his thumbs resting outside on the blue denim, and he was smiling that wonderfully warm smile of his.

Mike, David Webster and I had a nice time today, I said in my heart, holding the picture on a level with my face. *You'd like David. Please understand that my spending today with him and dating him next Friday doesn't mean I've stopped loving you, but he and I will be friends. And I need a friend, Mike. I do.*

WILDFIRE

Move from one breathtaking romance to another with the #1 Teen Romance line in the country!

NEW WILDFIRES! $1.95 each

- ☐ MU32539-6 **BLIND DATE** Priscilla Maynard
- ☐ MU32541-8 **NO BOYS?** McClure Jones
- ☐ MU32538-8 **SPRING LOVE** Jennifer Sarasin
- ☐ MU31930-2 **THAT OTHER GIRL** Conrad Nowels

BEST-SELLING WILDFIRES! $1.95 each

- ☐ MU31981-7 **NANCY AND NICK** Caroline B. Cooney
- ☐ MU32313-X **SECOND BEST** Helen Cavanagh
- ☐ MU31849-7 **YOURS TRULY, LOVE, JANIE** Ann Reit
- ☐ MU31566-8 **DREAMS CAN COME TRUE** Jane Claypool Miner
- ☐ MU32369-5 **HOMECOMING QUEEN** Winifred Madison
- ☐ MU31261-8 **I'M CHRISTY** Maud Johnson
- ☐ MU30324-4 **I'VE GOT A CRUSH ON YOU** Carol Stanley
- ☐ MU32361-X **THE SEARCHING HEART** Barbara Steiner
- ☐ MU31710-5 **TOO YOUNG TO KNOW** Elisabeth Ogilvie
- ☐ MU32430-6 **WRITE EVERY DAY** Janet Quin-Harkin
- ☐ MU30956-0 **THE BEST OF FRIENDS** Jill Ross Klevin
